A CAT'S GUIDE TO BONDING WITH DRAGONS

Dragoncat Book 1

CHRIS BEHRSIN

Edited by
WAYNE M. SCACE

To Lion. Betcha never expected you'd inspire a novel.

THE TOWER

My story doesn't start, unfortunately, in the hills of South Wales where I once had a good life, dashing through the long dry summer grass chasing butterflies with the heat from the sun beating against my fur.

It doesn't start eating salty tuna straight out of the can every Sunday morning, and the remains of roasted chicken in the afternoon.

Nor does it start with me propped up against a velvet cushion that was tossed onto the sofa as I watched Tom chasing Jerry on television, amazed and slightly offended at how stupid the creators made Tom.

Instead, it starts on a muggy day, where the only way of telling the weather was the pressure on the sides of my head and the moisture I could sense in my whiskers.

It starts in a stone tower with no windows, built of roughly hewn stones, sealed together with magic rather than mortar.

It starts trapped under the service of an evil warlock who teleported me into a world and back to a time where humans only kept cats like me to chase mice and rats.

I'm not a usual cat, either in these magical lands or my original home.

I'm a Bengal, meaning I'm larger than your average house cat. But not as large as a Savannah cat, two of whom inhabited my previous neighbourhood. Nor am I as large as that beast of a cat called a Maine Coon that I saw once on television – that was the biggest domestic cat I'd ever seen. But I am a descendant of the great Asian leopard cat, which makes me special in my own right.

My fur is a kind of amber colour, and I have these black patches on me. If you caught a leopard cub in the warm light of sunset, maybe I'd look a little similar. Except I'm not quite as lazy as a leopard, and not quite so stupid as to start a fight with a wildebeest. Also, don't mistake me for a tabby, a calico, or a tortoiseshell – those are the three worst things you can call a Bengal. I'm proud of my heritage and the way I look.

I have a name, but there's no way you'll be able to pronounce it in your language. You think Russian's hard, then try hissing and sputtering and mewling out one of our long names. The humans called me Ben as I'm a Bengal, imaginative as they were. The younger kid had a little more imagination and decided that because of my breed I should be called Bengie.

He was cute, that one, when he didn't try throwing me around the room.

I won't tell you much more about my life back in Wales, because it's probably uninteresting to human ears. Instead, I'll tell you about the evil warlock who whisked me away across time and space from a nutritious breakfast of milk and salmon trimmings right into the centre of a pentagram drawn in red chalk on his floor.

His name was Astravar, though I only learned of his name later. Like many men of misery, he liked to keep himself neat, not letting a single bobble of fluff grace his purple cloak, and always ensuring his collar kept as straight as still water. He had a long face, so gaunt you could see the bones underneath his eyes, cheeks, and chin. He had cruel grey eyes without a tint of colour in them – incredibly unnatural for a human.

At first, I looked up at him in shock. Then I thought, *might as well make the most of it.* Maybe at least I could get this strange man to pet me. So, I mewled for a little comfort, and you know what he did? He slapped me in the face.

I was quick to react, and I swiped at him with my right paw, scratching through his trousers. That was when he dragged me over to this tiny and cramped cage, and he locked me in there for two days straight without food and water. At least I think it was two days – there was no way of telling when day moved to night in that place.

When Astravar went out, I remained there in complete darkness, so cramped I couldn't even pace, my paws cold against the floor, without a blanket for comfort; where I could just feel the cockroaches crawling all over my paws and I couldn't do anything about them.

Those were the worst two days of my life.

You can probably imagine the rest of my life there wasn't easy, either. Astravar eventually let me out of the cage, but he never let me outside, and he kept the room so pitch black when he went out during the day, that I couldn't see a thing, even with cat vision.

Meanwhile, I would lie there on the thin mattress on the bedstead in this circular room, mewling away, hoping someone would pass by this tower, take pity, and knock down the door and steal me away. All the dust in here just made me sneeze all the time. Astravar didn't leave food in a bowl on the floor. Not even that cheap processed meat stuff – not that they had it in his day – and I couldn't help but long for the tuna, salmon, and roasted chicken and other delicious feasts that my previous owners would spoil me with every day. He didn't even leave proper water down, just some algae infested swill from the bottom of some dirty pond.

In all honesty, I don't know where he got the water from. Maybe it had magical properties. Maybe if I drank enough of it, I'd be able to grow wings and fly. But where would I go? Like I said, this tower didn't have any windows, so I couldn't even sit on the sill and gaze out at the wilderness.

Astravar often went out foraging during this time, and he'd come back with a bag full of things like mandrake roots, deadly nightshade, and all kinds of other plants you wouldn't dare touch with a paw, let alone a whisker.

Other days he'd bring back heavy shiny rocks like the one that hung above his enchantment table. Each time, he'd bring home all this stuff for who knows what nefarious intention, and he didn't even think to throw in a sprig of catnip.

Then, he'd work under the light of a transparent crystal above a stone table, engraved with red, yellow, and purple runes. This crystal hung too far out of reach for me to access, unfortunately. It would shine bright white, allowing him to get to work grinding his herbs with a mortar and pestle, etching more runes into the table, and hammering at shiny rocks; making a racket far too intense for my sensitive ears.

It wasn't terrible living in Astravar's tower for the first week or so. There were mice here, lots of them. Mind you, with the way this place had been put together, with stones thrown one on top of the other, there were plenty of places for mice to hide.

They hid in holes underneath the spinning wheel, behind the cold obsidian stone of the enchantment table, underneath the bed frame – full of nasty splinters, that one. There was even one in the pantry, which is the worst place to have a mouse hole, if you ask me. Particularly in a world where they haven't yet invented tin cans.

That's probably why Astravar summoned me here and, being a good cat, I got rid of them pretty quickly. I even ate a few of them, because I was hungry. Mouse tastes okay, but I can't stand all those sharp bones in awkward places. To be honest, I also prefer my meat cooked.

You would have thought a wizard would be selective about who he brought into his abode. Well, he was really, other than the mice, and the cockroaches, and the single rat who made it up there one morning. The rat didn't find his way through a hole, a window – because I already told you there weren't any – or even the front door. It found its way through a portal that Astravar summoned in that same pentagram he'd brought me through, bang in the centre of the tower.

Oh, and I didn't tell you it was a demon rat. That's right, a demon rat that I had to kill nine times. But that demon rat was only the first of them. After I had killed it, Astravar seemed to think it a good idea to summon more of them from his portals. Each day, after returning from his foraging, he'd enter his pentagram and mutter some strange words. Then the portal would open up, only for a few seconds mind, but it was enough for those infernal rats to swarm out of them. Then, I'd have to go chasing after them, and beating them down. It was exhausting, I tell you. By the end of it all, I just wanted to collapse on the bed.

Then, Astravar would sweep them all into some kind of open closet that he never let me anywhere near. Really, he must have picked up thousands of those demon rats after a while, and their bodies never seemed to decay.

I got no rewards for my efforts, no extra smoked salmon or chicken liver or anything like that. Trust me, I really didn't want to be eating any of those demon rats.

Anyway, here I am rabbiting on – don't you just love rabbits? – about the terrible life I had in the tower, when I have so much else to tell.

My story really starts one day when Astravar came home from his foraging. He'd just been picking some kind of mushrooms from a nearby cave, and the spores must have made him a little drowsy. So, he neglected to close the door properly.

I admit it, I thought twice about sneaking out the door, as I wasn't sure how long the mushrooms' spell would last on Astravar. If he woke up and saw that his prized Bengal was missing, he might hunt me down and turn me into a mouse or a frog, and then feed me to another cat.

Perhaps even one he teleported across time and space to hunt the demon rats he accidentally let through his portals. He'd probably pick an even bigger cat, just because Astravar liked to be ironic. I'm guessing he'd choose a Maine Coon.

But then it would be an equally fitting end to die of starvation in some conceited warlock's tower, and that thought made me bat open the heavy wooden door with my paw, slide out the gap, and make my way down the cold, stone, spiral staircase. I squeezed through the cold iron bars of the gate at the bottom of the tower, and I sprinted out into a cruel and unfamiliar world.

2

THE SPRINT

I didn't just run; I sprinted like a jaguar. I let my two hind legs carry me across the ground, imagining myself back in the jungles my ancestors came from, or dashing across the plains like the cheetahs the Savannah cats from my South Wales clowder claimed inhabited their ancestral lands. I didn't halt once to look over my shoulder, mind. There's no better way to kill momentum than to stop looking where you're going and then tumble into a rock or trip over a lump in the ground.

A strange purple mist enveloped the land, smelling more of death and decay than anything natural. The air here felt almost choking, and I found it difficult to breathe. But still, I soldiered on.

The ground beneath me wasn't great for running. It was marshy and cold. The water came up to my knees in places. Under normal circumstances, I wouldn't go near such a place, even if I knew a vast field of catnip lay on the other side of it. But then, anywhere was better than that tower.

My legs got tired after a while, but I didn't stop. I doubted that the mage could outrun me, but he might send something after me that could – a demon cheetah, perhaps. Or he could even use that portal to cross time and space and materialise right in front of me. I didn't know which possibility I feared more.

Fortunately, nothing came, and soon enough I managed to get out of the terrifying place. The sun also broke out of a thick grey layer of clouds. The sensation of warmth against my fur and naked nose, after so long without it, caused me to slow a little. I found myself on much firmer ground, thick with long dry grass and rich in pollen. Dragonflies buzzed around overhead, and I spent a little while chasing some of them. But, after running for so long, I tired quickly, and so I lay down to have a little snooze in the sun.

It was then that I noticed something wheeling by overhead. Now, back in South Wales, our little clowder had a rule. Everything that flew was good for hunting as soon as it landed. We didn't have eagles or hawks or anything like that in South Wales, so nothing in the sky would get us into any danger, except perhaps an occasional aggressive seagull.

But the thing that cast a shadow over me was enormous, to say the least. Even being whiskers knows how many miles up in the sky, it still looked bigger than me.

It had these long wings like those of a goose, but much broader and webbed rather than feathered. As it passed by, it let off a roar that cut apart the sky. The creature had come from a snow-capped mountain range in the distance, much more impressive than the Brecon Beacons back in Wales.

I yawned, deciding that as long as that creature didn't mind me, I wouldn't mind it either. So, I closed my eyes, and I slept fitfully, occasionally waking from nightmares of Astravar dropping out of a portal and putting me in that horrible cage again. But after a while, the dreams also faded away, and I awoke underneath the amber glow of the setting sun, which caused the high strands of grass around me to cast long shadows.

That was when I decided it was a good idea to go hunting. I wasn't sure what I was in the mood for then. But regardless, there was no running water nearby so I wouldn't have a chance of catching any fish. Unless I went back to the marshland, of course, which I wasn't going to do for obvious reasons. I tried chasing some starlings, but they lifted themselves up from the ground whenever I got within a few yards of them. Instead, I scouted around for voles or mice.

That's the thing though – small rodents are easy to hunt indoors. You just trap them inside their holes and scoop them out with a paw. But outside, they had places to run to, so the tiny critters would just scramble away.

After a while of stalking across the land looking for food, I came across a rock over what looked like moist ground, just next to an oak tree. I was desperate, so I turned it over, to find it crawling with earthworms and woodlice. They didn't make for a particularly appetizing meal – I hated eating creepy crawlies. But they satisfied the hunger pangs somewhat.

That was how I lived for the next several days or so. Eating insects and worms from underneath the earth, carrying on across the land hungry and tired, but at least grateful to once again be able to see the sun rise and set. I tried to travel and hunt at night. But the night didn't reward my hunting. I could swear there was something about the mice and rabbits here – they just knew to stay well away from me, as if they had greater dangers to deal with than a mere cat. They dug deeper into their burrows and curved their holes down into the ground so I couldn't reach into them successfully.

During the day, I slept in the long grass. Occasionally, one of those strange and massive beasts flying overhead would wake me from my slumber – always either going to or coming from the mountains, and always flying in the same direction.

When I saw them from the right angle, I would imagine something was sitting on top of them. Perhaps a human in bright clothing. But I thought it must be my imagination. I was hallucinating, and it wouldn't do me any good.

After a while of living this way, and the intense hunger pang in my stomach, I could literally feel my ribs pressing out against my chest. I realised my problem then. I needed to be around humans, and I'd lived without them for far, far too long.

It was ridiculous, I know. A great beast like me – a Bengal – not being able to hunt for himself. But I had to face the facts. I was domesticated, not bred to live in such a wild world.

Yet there was no way I would turn back to the marshlands to live with Astravar. Whiskers, if I returned there asking for food and a ticket back to my owners in South Wales, he'd probably skin me alive. Still I had no idea where I would find a town, or a city, or any place where I could find a nice family to feed me. I only had one lead – the massive creatures that flew overhead, always coming from one direction towards the mountains in the morning and returning the other way in the evening.

It was then that I decided that I'd follow their trail and find out where they were all returning to.

3

THE CASTLE

The trail led me to a mound, with what looked like a castle on top of it. Back in South Wales, we had a castle nearby on top of a hill. But while the one back home was in ruins, with stones that had crumbled apart hundreds of years ago and no one living there save for the occasional badger and hedgehog, this castle was teeming with life.

It wasn't ruined for a start, and had these tall towers, six of them, in fact, that rose up into the fluffy grey clouds, vanishing behind them. Those flying creatures wheeled around the towers and, once I was close enough, I saw them to be massive flying lizards with long necks and tails. They were like nothing I'd seen before, really, not even on the television.

Some beasts were red, some yellow, some green, some purple, some black, and some white. They flew in these brilliant aerobatic patterns that I could swear would put a swallow to shame. They dived through the clouds, almost touching the castle walls with their claws, before sharply veering upwards in the air.

It was then, watching from a slight rise with a cooling breeze passing through my fur, that I saw humans were riding these things. They carried long staffs across their backs, with crystals just like the ones Astravar used to collect, affixed onto the top of them. Sometimes, they took their short swords out of the sheaths at their hips, raised them up in the air, and swooped down with them. Other times, one of them would lift the staff off of their back, point it at the ground, and bathe the earth in brilliant displays of lightning, fire, and ice.

I'd never seen anything that could do that. I mean, back in South Wales, they had blocky machines that could create ice and blocky machines that could create fire. But they had to be closed to do so, and these staffs were creating brilliant effects all by themselves. I had to be dreaming.

I also found the behaviour of these people incredibly strange, even for humans. I mean, if you wanted to fly a creature like that, I would think you'd use it to get food. But they didn't seem to be trying to kill anything, but just attacking the ground and making pretty patterns on it. They brought nothing back from their hunts, not even a mouse.

None of it made any sense.

I tried to ignore them, as I realised a place with so many people in it would also likely have a kitchen with lots of food. In fact, I could smell the aroma of some smoked fish coming from somewhere within.

I sprinted towards the castle. The grass shortened as I approached, and I passed a stable with horses grazing outside. A scruffy-looking man was outside with the horses, tossing hay to one side of the wooden fence with a pitchfork. He had a strand of straw in his mouth, with smelly smoke rising from the tip.

The man glanced at me as I passed and uttered something. Not being human, of course, I didn't understand. I imagined he said something like, "Not seen too many of you fellows lately. We need a good mouser in the kitchens." But I have no evidence to suggest whether or not that is true.

For all I know, he could have accused me of being one of the demon incarnations that Astravar had summoned up from his portals. Although the man didn't seem afraid of me or anything like that.

I passed over an open drawbridge, and I stopped before I stepped underneath the portcullis. There was water in the moat, and I hadn't drunk a drop all day. I lowered myself down the bank – steep for humans but not for cats – and I lapped up several mouthfuls of the freshest water I'd tasted for months. It had a tint of rose in it and was strangely warm.

Several moments later, thoroughly hydrated, I found my way into the castle proper. There were people in there, hundreds of them. Some of them were sitting on a stone wall eating apples. Others, in pairs, sparred with each other with wooden swords – for who knows what reason. A man stood in the centre of the sword-wielders, shouting out at the top of his voice in a punctuated rhythm.

He was loud, and so I didn't want to go anywhere near him. Instead, I passed through the courtyard and pushed my way through a heavy looking door which was only slightly ajar. The corridors were cold and dusty, but I could smell my goal. The aroma of food was more intense than a chicken roast fresh out of the oven.

There was fish, there was chicken, there was pork, there was beef, and I swear I even caught the whiff of rosemary. I entered the kitchen, ducking between the feet of men and women scurrying around. I found a rather stout looking woman stirring something in a pot over a fire. I mewled at her, purring deep within my chest, and she turned and looked at me. Her expression suddenly turned to one of disdain, and she shouted out something at me.

She kicked me, and I shrieked back at her, and swiped with my paw, ripping through the fabric of her trousers. She shouted out at me again, and lurched at me with the spoon, dripping hot specks of a yellow mustardy sauce. But I darted away before she could hit me, finding my way between tangled feet and under the table.

I couldn't find any scraps of food on the floor, so I scurried out of the kitchens, and around the castle, looking out for a plate of something, sniffing around as I did. I stopped to spray a few times, of course, to let other cats know that a Bengal was now interested in this territory.

Soon enough, I found another door, with some steps leading up a thin spiral staircase. I followed this upward and took the next room out, to find another straight and dusty corridor. Along the left-side edges of it, the stone peeled away into massive chambers. I turned into the first one, and I found a massive deer's carcass half-eaten on the floor, set in front of an opening, looking out towards the mountains in the distance. The brown roasted meat emitted this amazing smoky scent that drew me towards it like a magnet draws iron filings.

I was so hungry I didn't even bother to check what else might be in the room. I sprinted over to the meat, tore an enormous chunk off one of its ribs and started chewing it apart on the floor.

Then, there came a clear voice in my head. I'd never heard such a language before, but I understood it as clear as bowl-water. It was as if a human was speaking inside my mind, and I could put meaning to every single word.

"What in the Seventh Dimension do you think you are doing, youngling?"

But that voice couldn't have belonged to anything, surely. I was starving and clearly hearing things.

"You dare ignore a creature of magic... Look behind you, you fool." I felt a sudden searing sensation of heat passing over my head, and a jet of flame hit the wall right in front of me.

I shivered, and then I turned around and shrieked out of shock, as hackles thrust out of my arched back. I looked right into a massive yellow eye, set into a red reptilian head which must have been around five times the size of me, if not more.

"Finally," the voice said. It sounded like a female human, yet still low-pitched at that. *"Now, I'm starting to see some well-deserved respect."*

AN UNEXPECTED FIND

I didn't know how to react to the beast that had somehow just spoken to me in my head. Up close, it was like a creature out of nightmares I'd never imagined possible. It looked even more terrifying than the demon cheetah I'd imagined Astravar might have sent hunting me.

The only lizard-like creatures I'd seen before were the newts and salamanders back in my former owners' garden back home. I would chase them through the grass sometimes, never really intending to kill them – they didn't look particularly appetizing, and so I'd release them and let them scurry back into the water, and then I'd go back to chasing butterflies instead.

But I'd seen crocodiles on television, with their macabre grins and ability to lurch out at people from the water. This beast was like a crocodile, except worse. She had sharp teeth along the side of her mouth, eyes that glowed bright yellow like miniature suns, huge front-loaded nostrils that didn't just steam but smoked, a breath that stank like rotting meat, and this strange fire burning at the back of her throat whenever she opened her mouth.

Not to mention her sheer enormity. My first thought upon seeing her was that she must have had enough of the deer and now wanted to eat me for dinner. What I didn't consider at the time was that she would probably hate eating me for the same reason I hated eating mice.

I backed up all the way to the drop and looked down at the landscape below. I was far too high up to jump down without injuring myself – even with my ability to land on all fours.

"*Oh, come on, I can't surely be that scary,*" the creature said, again inside my mind. "*I'm only a Ruby, after all.*"

But what was I meant to say back? I mean, normally I shouldn't understand another species' language. Yet, here I was hearing her in my head as if she was now part of my train of thought. I hissed back at her, looking for a way to dart back out the door. But she had blocked off any chance of escape.

"*You know, cats aren't usually allowed outside their cattery,*" she said, and she raised one of her massive brows. She was hairless and had these harsh red scales that seemed to converge towards her eyes. "*Sometimes, the humans let them out in the kitchens. But no one in their right mind would enter a dragon's chambers. So how, might I ask, did you end up here? Or is this your first time visiting Dragonsbond academy? Perhaps you're a stray from outside.*"

I arched my back even higher than I thought possible, and hissed again at the creature, baring my teeth. In hindsight, I don't know how I was expecting to scare her. But then the fact I hadn't eaten for days meant I was a little grumpy and wasn't thinking straight.

"*I've never known your kind to be so unfriendly. Don't you speak at all? I've given you the honour of having access to my mind, and I thought you'd at least say something.*"

Well, I'd never spoken to any creature that wasn't a cat before. But surely it was just the case of putting one word after the other in my mind. I tried it.

"*What are you?*" I asked. Really, given the circumstances, she couldn't expect me to be a creature of many words.

The massive lizard tossed her head forward and let out a massive roar that almost sent me stumbling off the wall. "*What am I? How dare you suggest you've never heard of a dragon.*"

"*A what?*" Come to think of it, I think they had called the Maine Coon 'Dragon' on television, funny as humans were with names.

"*A dragon... you know, fearsome creatures who knights used to hunt down with lances and swords. Or at least they did until the warlocks rose to power and became both ours and the humans' arch enemies.*"

I opened my eyes wide at the creature. For a moment, I didn't feel threatened but rather utterly confused.

"*Are you really telling me you've never heard of a dragon? You don't have nightmares of us in the night? You don't tremble when you see us, the fiercest of all the creatures known to man?*"

"*I... Are you like a hippopotamus?*" Word had it from the two Savannah cats in my old neighbourhood, that these were the fiercest of all the creatures. The two cats had never seen a hippopotamus, of course. Such creatures didn't roam the wilds of South Wales. But their ancestors had passed down the wisdom to fear the hippopotamus, monsters of the mud with razor sharp buck teeth.

The dragon creature bellowed out again, and this time a little heat came out with the roar, making me think it might finally cook me as it had probably done the venison. "*How dare you compare me to a hippo – a hippa – sorry, what was that word, again?*"

"A hippopotamus," I replied.

"*How dare you compare me to a hippopotamus.*"

"*Do you even know what a hippopotamus is?*"

She raised one of her massive eyebrows, and steam puffed out of her nose. "*No... Enlighten me.*"

I explained to her exactly what the Savannah cats had told me. As I did, I kept glancing over at the ground below, wondering if I could survive the leap, because this insult would probably be the straw that broke the dragon's temper. Now, she would likely tear me to shreds.

She puffed out a second plume of smoke from her nostrils, this one much thicker than the first. It hit me right in the face. I coughed, then I sneezed, and I prepared myself to jump. But instead, the dragon made some strange low-pitched noise. After a moment, I recognised this as laughter.

"Is that what you think dragons do? We wallow about in the mud all day? I've never heard anything so ridiculous in over fifty years."

"Then what do you do?" I asked.

She shook her head. *"You know, you've been quite entertaining, and I hear that you cats have quite good balance. Why don't I take you on a little ride?"*

The dragon lowered her head to the ground, and then the arch of her back followed. This was the first time I saw the spikes running along her back. They followed two thin rows on either side of her spine, curling out and then back in as if part of a second ribcage. But fortunately, they were so close together, it didn't look like I'd tumble out from between them.

"What are you doing?" I asked. She'd gone from wanting to eat me to now deciding to go to sleep in front of me.

"I've only just come of age as a dragon," she continued, *"and I've reached the time of my life where I'm due to choose a rider. But these spikes present a problem. With them, I can't hold a saddle. They're such a nuisance to the humans, that they've threatened to cut them off. But I'm proud of my spikes and I don't want to have them cut off. Now, maybe, you could be a solution."*

"What the whiskers are you talking about?" I asked.

"Just hop on my back, and we'll go for a little ride. If it goes well, maybe I'll let you have a little venison for supper."

Now that was an offer I couldn't refuse. I looked over at the carcass, the delicious smoky scent of it wafting into my nostrils. *"Let me have a bite first. Then I'll consider."*

"You drive a hard bargain," the dragon replied. *"So let it be. But only a bite, unless your tail wants to see the end of my flames."*

I cautiously approached the deer, eyeing the dragon on the way. It seemed to pose no threat, so I took hold of a bite of the roast in my teeth and sequestered it away to the other end of the room.

After I'd eaten it from the floor, I decided that maybe this dragon creature wouldn't be so bad after all. So I did what she said. I leaped over her nose, landed on her forehead, and then I nestled myself between the spikes on her back.

Suddenly, the ground lurched underneath me, although this ground wasn't composed of earth but dragon flesh. But her spikes held me firmly in place, as she walked me over to the edge.

Presently, the dragon unfurled her massive wings, sending up a massive gust of wind around me. Then, I almost tumbled backwards down the corridor between her two rows of spikes, but I found my footing before I rolled off onto the floor.

"*Keep steady,*" the dragon said.

"*Of course I'm steady. I'm a cat,*" I replied.

"*We shall see,*" the dragon replied, and before I knew it, the skin underneath me spasmed in a sickening way that made me want to vomit. Presently, her feet lifted off the ground, and she carried me up into the sky.

5

DECISIONS

I had never seen the ground beneath me so far away. It was so distant it looked unreal, as if it was part of a painted floor, so flat that I could just leap on to it. Fortunately, other parts of my body told me that this wasn't a good idea. My balance centre told me to stay nestled safely in the corridor between the dragon's rows of spikes. Then, there was the noise of the wind whooshing around me, creating an intense chill that cut right through my short fur coat.

Part of me wished I hadn't leapt on this massive creature's back. I thought that within a minute, or perhaps even thirty seconds, I'd be a pancake on the grasslands below. Perhaps that was how dragons liked to eat cats – break all their bones first to tenderise the meat a little.

I also didn't like the way the dragon sent me tumbling between her spikes with every sudden sharp manoeuvre. Cats are made to stay on their feet, not to be flung around like a hamster that had just fallen unconscious on its wheel.

After a while, she stopped whirling around so much, and I felt sick. I tried to find some balance, but with each step I was incredibly dizzy. I tried to jump up on the dragon's head to at least get a good view of the horizon. But the wind roared even louder up there, and the way the ground moved below just didn't look right. That feeling in the back of my head told me to stay well away from the edges. So, I retreated down the dragon's neck and cowered within her corridor of spikes.

"My name is Salanraja," the dragon said after a while, *"and I'm a creature born of magic."*

"You say some strange things," I replied. *"Can't we have a conversation about food?"*

"Not until you've told me your name."

I tried to swallow down the nausea and vertigo spinning inside my head and put some word to thought. *"My name's Ben,"* I said.

"What a mundane name."

"You wouldn't be able to pronounce my actual name."

"And you wouldn't be able to pronounce my magical name either, and I wouldn't give it to you before a thousand suns had burned. But, for your common name, you could at least have thought of something with a little appeal. Perhaps you have another name?"

"Don't tell me you want to start calling me Bengie too..."

"Bengie..." Salanraja paused for a moment. *"That at least is passable."*

"But I hate that name."

"It's far better than Ben," Salanraja said.

I hissed at the dragon, and I tried to dig my claws into her back, but its skin was far too leathery between the scales to even injure her. I don't think she noticed, to be honest, which was probably fortunate for me. *"I didn't pick my name,"* I said after a moment.

"Oh, so who did?"

"The humans."

That was when I felt her belly rumble, and out of her mouth came that maniacal laughter again. *"You let the humans name you? I never realised cats had so little self-respect."*

"What does a name matter? All I need is a familiar word the humans can call so I know when I'm getting food."

"It matters more than you can imagine," Salanraja replied. *"A well-chosen name will make you remembered to both your enemies and your friends. You don't hear people saying, 'Excuse me, which Salanraja was that', do you?"*

"To be honest, I've never heard anyone use the name Salanraja at all."

"That will change. Once I strike my legacy into the hearts of men and dragons. It will become a name remembered throughout the history textbooks. One that all sentient creatures on this planet will utter in both fear and respect."

I yawned. At least when Salanraja talked to me, she stopped those crazy flight manoeuvres. So, it seemed better to keep the conversation going.

"You really are full of yourself, aren't you?" I said.

"I'm a dragon. The greatest creature in the lands. What do you expect?"

"A little modesty, perhaps. It would go a long way."

"And what do you know about modesty?"

I licked my beautiful, silky fur. *"Look. I know that you're big and strong, and all that. But also, quite frankly, you're ugly. Fair enough, you might scare people, but somehow I doubt you have the grace or intellect of a cat."*

"Grace?" Salanraja's body rumbled from beneath my feet and she let out a massive roar once again. *"I shall show you grace."*

Just when I thought I had my balance mastered, Salanraja's body lurched once again. She threw me to the left, and then she spun me around and around as if I was trapped in a washing machine. I don't know how long the dragon had me tumbling around in that corridor within her spikes. But, once she levelled out, I felt as if every bone had broken in my body. I also wanted to throw up.

"That's not graceful," I pointed out. *"It's no wonder none of the humans ever want to ride you if you keep behaving like that."*

The dragon turned her massive head back to me. Her leathery top lip had curved upwards in a snarl, displaying a long fang-like incisor that was yellowing a little at the top. *"And you're probably now going to show me what graceful is,"* Salanraja said.

Whiskers! She would have to make such a request after beating me around so much. *"I can show you graceful. If you promise not to drop me out of the sky."*

"Be my guest."

I stretched out my limbs and back, feeling my bones creak as I did so. Then, I tested the spot in front of me on Salanraja's back first, before climbing up her neck and onto her head. I perched myself there, half worried that the dragon would throw me off at any second, but instead she made a deep rumbling sound that almost sounded like a purr.

I looked down at the ground rolling by below, the fields arranged in uneven squares of green and yellow, trees dotted between them. A layer of fluffy clouds passed by overhead. I didn't particularly want to be up here in the cold wind, and I tried not to pay attention to the ground whirling by below.

"You are sitting on my head," she said.

"I don't intend to stay up here," I replied. "I just wanted to prove my point."

"Which is?"

"That I made it up here without causing you any pain at all. Grace is all about being able to pass through an environment without disturbing it. That way, we can sneak past even the scariest of dogs undetected. It's about elegance, not breaking every bone in your passenger's body."

"My flight might have felt ungraceful to you, but it would have looked spectacular to an observer on the ground."

"And do you see any observers down there? I see a few sheep. But their eyes are for the grass they're munching, and not you."

Salanraja laughed again, but this time it came out as a low chuckle, probably because maniacal laughter would result in throwing me right off my perch. "You know, I never thought I'd meet someone suitable. But you've changed my mind. Get down from there," she said. "I want to show you something."

I scratched my head with my hind leg. "Tell me what it is first."

"Would you rather I threw you off my head and caught you on my back? I'm not always the best catch, I might warn you."

"No," I said, and I stalked back down her neck, nestling myself in the corridor of her back. "Just don't do any of that rough flying again. It's not good for my spine, flexible as it is."

She didn't seem to hear me. "Hold on for now," she said. "This is going to be a rough landing."

"Hold on to what?"

"Anything you can find."

Though the air was cold before, it now carried icy blasts and I felt like my fur was going to freeze. Ahead, the snow-capped mountain range I saw before was approaching, the sun glistening off the glazed tops of it, with eagles – and this time I mean birds and not dragons – wheeling over a blanket of mountain mist.

Salanraja roared up to the sky, and then she reeled backwards. She used the momentum to pull herself upwards, and the chill in the air intensified. Suddenly, she decelerated. I shrieked as I rolled down the corridor of spikes towards Salanraja's head. Beneath that was a blanket of caked snow, coming at us faster and faster.

"Stop!" I said to her in my head.

"I said, hold on," Salanraja replied.

I had no choice but to comply, because I almost tumbled off her neck. But I caught myself last minute. The spikes that ran up the back of her neck were made of a soft kind of ivory, and I managed to dig my claws into one, and hold myself there with all my strength, as I dangled above the snowfield. I thought for a moment that I would plummet with such a force I'd cause an avalanche.

Salanraja thudded into the ground with such impact, I got thrown off her neck into the snow. Luckily, of course, I landed on my feet. But once I felt the cold, powdery stuff against them, I shrieked and ran leaped right back up onto Salanraja's back.

"What's the matter?" Salanraja asked.

I shuddered. *"I hate snow,"* I said. *"I hate it more than I hate rain."*

Salanraja barked out a laugh into the icy wind. *"Don't be such a wimp. You have that thick fur coat. What about me? What do I have to keep me warm?"*

"Dragon fire?"

"True that," Salanraja replied. *"Well, we're here."* She lifted up a claw and pointed to a cave mouth tall enough to accommodate nine stacked elephants.

"And where is here, exactly?" I asked.

"This is the source of our world's magic. It's a place where all dreams are

first born before they travel through the ley lines of the land into the minds of mindful beings. Here dragons first get their fire, and dragon riders first get their gifts. This is only one of thousands of entrances in a place we guard against the warlocks and dark creatures that wish to use it for ill."

I yawned widely and scratched my neck with my hind paw. *"Okay, okay, it's special. I've got that. But what is it? Get to the point, will you?"*

Salanraja shook her head. But this time, she decided not to complain about my rudeness. *"It's the Versta Caverns of the Crystal Mountains, and here you shall learn of your destiny. Because I don't know why, but my gut is telling me to choose you as my next rider. I think we are destined for great things together, Bengie, and legends say that we dragons can foretell the future."*

6

MADE OF CLAY

The Versta Caverns were perhaps the most spectacular thing I'd ever seen. I used to think birds were fascinating to watch. But these caverns, which seemed a massive passageway into the bowels of the earth, contained gems as large as houses and which shone out in every single imaginable colour. Within them, the swirling patterns of light seemed to depict images so surreal they might as well be dreams. If I stared at one long enough, I imagined I was seeing myself in a familiar world that I'd seen in the Land of Nod.

In one of them, I saw myself from a distance, running through long grass, chasing dragonflies like I had been only days ago. I caught one in my paw until it bit me, and then I yelped out in pain. But after that, I was soon out there chasing another dragonfly, and this time I caught it and examined it, and it didn't seem to be a dragonfly at all, but a small red dragon. The dream zoomed in, to make the dragon bigger, until I could see myself flying on that dragon's back. The corridor of spikes had gone now, and I looked as comfortable there as I would on a garden fence.

I saw an enemy down below, something skeletal, with hollow ribs. I pointed downwards at it with my paw, and a column of fire came down from the sky, charring both creature and earth beneath.

"*Dragons aren't the only entities that can foretell the future,*" Salanraja told me, clearly realising what I was staring at. "*Sometimes these crystals display a creature's dreams. Sometimes they display premonitions. Sometimes, they show the past. And sometimes, rumour has it, they can even see across dimensions.*"

I sat on her back, as she stalked carefully through the cavern, as if with reverence for the crystals that lay within. Though the passage was wide enough for her to walk through, the ceiling came down too low for Salanraja to take off into the air and fly through the passageway, although I didn't discount the possibility there might be taller chambers as we ventured further through the caverns.

There was no snow in here, so I probably could have continued on foot. But I had reached the point where I, admittedly, was quite enjoying the ride. There was no snow on the red-packed earth that supported the crystals, and I could taste the clay in the air.

"*You can sit on my head if you want a better view.*" Salanraja said.

"*But won't it get hot up there if you decide to breathe fire?*" I replied.

"*Oh, you won't have to worry about that here. The crystals prevent me from using my magic.*"

I mewled, and ran up Salanraja's neck onto her head. Now, I could see everything in panorama. We'd already passed quite a way into the caverns and the entrance was getting increasingly smaller behind us. The crystals seemed to not just emanate life, but a glow that warmed me from the bones out. There was something about this place that I liked, and I didn't want to leave.

But then, Salanraja jerked to a halt. She wasn't going fast to begin with, but she was so massive that her sudden motion sent me tumbling forwards. Fortunately, I caught myself, so I didn't end up hanging off one of her nostrils. I didn't want to end up swinging right into her mouth.

"*Don't make a sound,*" Salanraja said. "*Not even a purr*"

How she could ever expect me to stop purring, I don't know. It was like asking a dog to stop wagging its tail. "*What is it?*"

"*There's something there, just around the corner...*"

I craned my head over Salanraja's top mounted horn to get a better look. But I couldn't see what she was fussing about.

"*Wait until it comes into the light of the crystals,*" Salanraja continued. "*It's camouflaged against the earth.*"

It didn't take me long to notice something out of place. On the draught came a whiff of rotten vegetable juice, as if someone had painted it over the clay.

I zoned in on the smell. Then I detected motion. True enough, something was slithering around down there, almost concealed. It moved in the shadows the crystal cast against the rocks in front of it, sliding over the ground, without making a footstep. It seemed as if it was part of the earth itself, growing out of it to move forward, and then shrinking back into the ground. It turned toward us and then I saw its two eyes. They were glowing, just like the crystals.

"*A golem,*" Salanraja said. "*Made of clay.*"

"A what?"

"*Do you know nothing of magical creatures?*"

"I knew nothing of this thing you called magic until today, and I still don't know exactly what it's meant to do."

Salanraja lowered her head to the ground, very slowly. "*A golem is a creation of man, a part of the earth given life through a magical crystal. It's probably here to mine crystals for a warlock's dark plans.*"

"I thought you said that we couldn't use magic in here."

"*We can't.*"

"Then how can a magical creature survive here?" I asked.

"*Because it would have been conjured outside. Those eyes are just one of a warlock's ways of seeing. The warlock in question is unlikely to notice us unless we do something to alert him or her to our presence. But its very existence here means that there is a warlock nearby.*"

"A warlock? Astravar..." The man had never told me his name, or if he had, I hadn't understood his language at the time to register it. But he'd burnished it into my memories through some kind of magic. Now, I could see his long face and cruel grey eyes inside my mind each time I remembered his name.

"It could be Astravar," Salanraja said, "or it could be any of the other six known warlocks to inhabit the Darklands."

"And what does he want with us? We're not doing him any harm..."

"Our kingdom of Illumine is at war with the warlocks whose souls have been consumed by dark magic. They strive for the destruction of all non-conjured life in this world. Humans, cats, and every other creature that you hunt and cherish would be annihilated if they had their way."

I glanced around at the shining massive gems, trying hard not to be mesmerised by their beauty. He'd had one of these swinging above him as he worked, filling his tower with light. Others he'd used to summon demons from portals. Whiskers, he'd probably summoned me from a portal using one of the crystals

"There's a crystal here for you, Bengie," Salanraja said. "As soon as I decided to choose you as my dragon rider, one of the crystals here called me. Now, you must find the one that knows you well, and it will give it your ability."

"My ability?"

"Of course. All dragon riders have a kind of magic about them, and as you grow as a dragon rider your crystal will grant you more abilities."

"I—" I couldn't believe my pointy ears. I hadn't even learned of magic before today. Now this 'dragon' was telling me I could use it. "What abilities will it give me?"

"You will only gain one for now, and you won't know what it is until you've gained it. Now, go and find your crystal, and do so silently, because we don't want to attract the attention of that golem."

I looked down at the morphing clay creature again, its form twisting from one wicked shape to the next. It kept moving forward in a direction, and its arm had moulded itself into the shaft of some tool. A metal blade had morphed out of the top of this, looking something like a pickaxe. The golem was shifting towards the crystal that I'd seen my dream in before. The one that seemed to know me well...

"I think I know which one's mine," I said.

"Oh?"

"The one with my dreams in it... It's that purple crystal over there."

"*What?*" Salanraja said, and her head tossed back all of a sudden, almost throwing me off it. "*No! The golem!*"

I could feel Salanraja was getting irate, and so I scrambled down her neck, so she didn't throw me on to the cold floor in her rage. Then, I turned around to see what she was screaming at. The golem now had that pickaxe-like tool raised over the crystal, and it looked like it was about to bring it down in a wide arc.

It was about, in other words, to smash my crystal to pieces.

7

SINKING

Salanraja bellowed out a roar, and the golem turned in a broad circle. It bent over backwards, then let out an ear-piercing screech that sent my head spinning for a moment.

"You can't let it destroy your crystal. You have to fight it," Salanraja said.

"How? It's bigger than a human, and it moves funny."

Salanraja lowered her head back to the floor. *"Knock out its eyes – and you'll destroy its magical energy."*

"Easy for you to say... Why don't you just eat it?"

"I can't, you fool. Just do it. We don't have much time."

Salanraja shook her head, like a dog shaking off water, sending me tumbling onto the floor. I landed right next to the golem, and I gazed up at it. The thing was massive, twice as large as a human perhaps, and twice as wide too. It stared down at me with its two crystal eyes – one red, one blue. It also had the pickaxe extension on its arm raised, which was swinging down towards me.

I screeched, and then I scrambled out of the way, as the pickaxe buried itself in the earth. It got stuck there for a moment, giving me time to recover myself. I tried scratching at the golem's leg, but my claws just went right through its body, bringing off some sticky clay that I tried to shake off but couldn't.

"Do something, Salanraja," I said.

"Like what? My claws will just go right through it, and they're much too large to dislodge his eyes. If I try eating it, it will just reform in my stomach and rip me apart from the inside."

"If it's made of clay, can't you just breathe fire on it? It might harden the thing, securing it in place."

"I can't use magic in here, remember, and even if I could, it would be disrespectful to the crystals. This is your job, Bengie. Accept it."

By the time Salanraja had finished explaining things, the golem had its pickaxe raised again, and was lifting it up into the air. Meanwhile, its other hand had grown into a scythe-like blade, also metallic. It swept this around in a low arc, and I leapt over it just in the nick of time and then stumbled over towards the wall.

"The eyes, Bengie. Go for the eyes," Salanraja said.

I snarled up at her, then darted behind a tall column of stone. I used that spot as my cover as I arched my back and hissed at my opponent. But this didn't stop it coming at me. It took a high swing with its scythe blade and cut right through the column. Then, the golem charged into the column with its shoulder, rocking it slightly, and then bringing it crashing down. I scampered out of the way to avoid getting flattened into the floor.

I ran in a circle, trying to get around the golem. It bent down towards me, evidently preparing itself to sweep that scythe blade around once again. I lowered myself, ready to pounce on it, but the golem's legs melted into the earth and rose again so fast I couldn't work out where to leap.

"You won't weaken it, Bengie," Salanraja said. *"It will just tire you out if you keep trying to evade it."*

"Can't we just run away?"

"No. Watch out!"

I turned to see the pickaxe almost upon my head. I rolled out of the way at the last second. Then I turned again and bared my teeth and I saw an opening. The golem's arm was right there on the ground, the pickaxe stuck in there. I darted forwards and leapt onto its shoulder and, before I slid back down, I swiped away the red crystal. It fell to the floor.

But before I could go for the other crystal, the golem's shoulder melted away underfoot. Its entire body dissolved into the earth. Next moment, it had formed a puddle with me at the centre. I started sinking down into the thick viscous pool. I tried to swim out towards the edge, but I just ended up getting dragged further and further down.

"It's eye, Bengie. Stop struggling, the eye's right in front of you."

I kept my head above the surface and tried to focus on what Salanraja was talking about. There was a crystal in front of me, glowing blue. I pawed at it, but the motion just sent me further into the puddle of clay. I was down to my neck at that point, just inches away from not being able to breathe.

Ah well, it had been a good life with more roasted salmon and chicken than I'd get in the wild.

"Bengie!" Salanraja called out.

She readied herself to roar, then she lowered her head into the clay and tried to lift me up using her front horn. But it was too slippery, and I couldn't get any purchase on it. I could still see the blue gem right in front of my eyes now. My claws were underneath the surface of the clay now. So, instead, I ducked my head forward, and I took a massive mouthful of earth and gem.

I'd never tasted clay before, but I'd had a few mouthfuls of soil in my kitten days when I'd needed to chew grass to help me bring back up furballs. This clay had the taste of soil, but not the texture. It was pretty gross.

My head sank underneath the surface of the clay. I tried not to breathe down there – the last thing I wanted was nostrils full of that stuff – and I kept my lips firmly shut.

But soon enough, my breath gave out, and I felt intense pressure on my eyes, as if I was going to black out. Then the earth shuddered beneath me. Next thing I knew, I was shooting out of the clay like a cannon. Or at least I thought I was.

What had actually happened was that Salanraja had reached down again and tossed me out with her horn, just as the clay started to harden around me. I flew across the passage, legs flailing, and then I hit my head against the wall.

"Quick Bengie, get on my back."

I tried to come to my senses, pretty dizzy. *"I thought we'd killed it,"* I said.

"We did, but the warlock will be after us. There'll be more of them."

I didn't need further instruction. Finally, we were getting out of here. I scrambled up onto Salanraja's back, trying to ignore the intense throbbing where my neck met my spine. Before we left, Salanraja lurched forward and wrapped her mouth around the crystal that had my dreams inside of it and charged away.

I ran down to the tail-end of her corridor of spikes to see what was going on behind me. I could only vaguely make out the shapes morphing against the rock in the background, but they seemed to be getting closer and closer.

But they didn't reach us in time before Salanraja was back out in the icy wind. She lifted herself up into the sky, and I almost fell off her tail, being so close to the end of it. I caught myself and scurried back up towards her neck.

From my vantage point, I looked down below, and I could see around a dozen golems against the snow, no longer camouflaged within their natural terrain. My head was spinning, and I couldn't look at them for very long.

That was the first time I'd ever heard him speak in a language I could understand. It was Astravar, speaking in my head. I recognised him from the voice's timbre…

"You!" he said. *"You ran away from my tower, you destroyed my golem, and now you steal away my magic. You may be just a cat, but I never let insults go unforgotten. Soon, I shall hunt you down, and then I will make you pay!"*

8

GIFT

I didn't pay too much attention to the journey. My head was absolutely spinning. It ached like it had never ached before, and any time I tried to move it in one direction, an intense thumping would cause me to lower my head back down again as a deep groan came out of my chest. But I remember the colours I saw – white segueing to yellow and green, blue sky rolling overhead, and the bright light from the sun exacerbating the pain in my head.

That journey felt like hours, and I didn't even have the energy to ask Salanraja where we were heading. Meanwhile, I kept remembering Astravar's voice in my head. It hadn't been my imagination, and it hadn't been the stuff of dreams, I was sure. Rather, his presence there had been much like Salanraja's – as if he could read what I was thinking and had known my very location. He must have been in the crystal that I'd swallowed – the eye of the golem – which already contained the warlock's magic.

Eventually Salanraja thudded against the ground. Because of my headache, I didn't have a great sense of balance, and so she ended up bashing me into the side of her corridor of spikes.

"*Wake up, Bengie,*" she said.

I didn't move from my position. Instead, I yawned widely. *"I told you that I hate that name,"* I replied.

"Bengie, this is important. Get off." The body underneath my chest shuddered like an earthquake, and I felt it starting to warm.

I growled at Salanraja, then I stood up and stretched, shaking every muscle in my body at the same time. It wasn't just my head that hurt, but my back and legs, and I couldn't take one step without some kind of pain lancing through my knees. I knew that if I didn't get off Salanraja, she'd shake me off. So I sauntered lazily down her tail to the ground, feeling every single stride within my joints.

"Why can't we just rest?" I asked.

"Just go to the crystal. It will sort out your ails and give you your gift. You've worked for this Bengie. Don't waste the opportunity now."

"Can't it give it to me later?" I asked. *"I'm tired. And, if you could bring me that venison you promised, I'd much appreciate it."* I lay down in the long grass. It wrapped around me, providing an extra blanket of warmth.

"No!" Salanraja let out a gigantic roar, causing me to leap to my feet in shock. I stared up at her and blinked, and she lowered her massive head to me and enveloped me in a plume of smoke from her nostrils. *"I didn't bring you all this way to show disrespect to the crystals. This is not just your future on the line, but also mine."*

"But the future is the future, like tomorrow is tomorrow. Now, this hour, I need to sleep."

Salanraja bared her sharp teeth at me, and a rumble came out from her belly. I could just imagine the fire burning within there. Her nostrils flared and her yellow eyes took on a brilliant glow.

"Fine," I said, and I walked around her towards the tall crystal she'd left on the ground. It was standing on its point, balancing there as if upheld by an invisible force. It was even taller than the statue I remembered on the roundabout back in South Wales – a weird metallic creature, formed of ribs that curved out from its centre like sickle blades.

My joints continued to ache with each step. My throat was also dry; probably all the moisture in it had been wicked away by that foul-tasting clay, and I imagined the feast of venison I could be eating right now.

But as I approached the crystal, these thoughts washed away, and I instead became mesmerised by the images flashing by behind the facets once again. My eyes fixated on the light emanating from within. The images displayed a version of me looking so much stronger than I'd ever imagined. I was atop Salanraja again, carrying some kind of staff in my mouth. Dark-winged creatures – that looked like a cross between a bat and a buzzard – flitted around us, and I had my eyes closed as purple tentacles of light lashed out from the glowing stone of the same colour at the staff's head.

The bats swooped down, extending out talons that were almost as long as their wings. But before they could get close, the tentacles whipped at them, and knocked them out of the sky. Hundreds of the creatures fell to the earth. Another swarm approached from the front, and Salanraja tossed back her head and let out a column of amber flame at them. When the light from the flame subsided, the creatures were nowhere to be seen.

"*This is your destiny, Ben,*" a voice said in my head. It sounded like a female human voice, but one I could understand. Just like the mistress back home in South Wales, it had a soft lilt to it, which drew me even further towards the crystal.

"*You have weaknesses, and you have fears; we all do. But the difference between those who live up to their callings and those who don't is that we don't let the weaknesses control us. Pride, sloth, reliance, and gluttony are transient. Yet, if you let them, they will stop you from becoming who you are meant to be.*"

I mewled, and I rubbed up against the crystal. When I touched it, its warmth seemed to cleanse away the muscle pains and my headache. I suddenly became aware of everything around me – the distant bird sounds, the swishing of the cool wind as it brushed through my fur, the slow rhythmic sound of Salanraja's breath, the clouds, the light flowing out of the crystal and soothing everything it touched.

Of course, because I was a cat, being aware of my environment was nothing new to me. But this was different. Before, I would react to every sudden movement, unable to control my instincts. Now, I could disconnect from it all, and focus on what I chose to be of value. I could decide consciously what was a threat and what was not.

I was completely in control of my own mind and body.

"*Why do I need this?*" I asked the crystal. "*Salanraja makes me think this is important, but I'm not sure what I'm meant to do.*"

"*That's because you don't know the fate of the world to come,*" the voice in the crystal said. "*It's not just our world, but many, including your own.*"

"*What do you mean?*"

"*Close your eyes, and I will show you.*"

I did as the crystal bade me to. I could still feel its presence, feel its warmth washing over me, and I turned into it as if turning my face to the sun. Then, I felt a slight pressure on my eyelids – not enough to be painful.

Behind them, the tapestry of the future began to unfurl.

9

A CAT'S PURPOSE

At first, I didn't think I was looking at the real world, but rather a moving painting. Still I recognised the setting – the crystal had taken me back to my home in South Wales. I didn't traverse it like a normal cat would, nor was I being carried on a dragon's back. Instead, I floated over the land, as if dreaming.

It was different to the world I'd grown up in and come to love. The landscape was charred; the rolling hills beneath contained no grass or trees, only settled dust. The sky wasn't blue but a deep blood red, spattered with a layer of purple cloud, from which came an occasional flash of lightning.

The vision floated me into the town. The streets had immense cracks in them, out of which fronds of spiky ochre weeds waved in the odorous breeze. The houses and bungalows, usually decorated with shiny quartz, were all reduced to rubble. I floated into my former owner's house, past the broken television set in the living room, into the kitchen where my food and water bowls lay shattered on the kitchen floor. In the bedroom were my owners, all three of them as skeletons huddled together on the master bed.

"If all good creatures succumb to superficial desires," the crystal said, "this is what shall come to pass. The warlocks' greed won't just stop on this *world, but it will cross dimensions. We crystals cannot control how creatures use our magic, but we can give you the powers to stop the evil of this world spreading across dimensions like a blight."*

I had nothing to say to that. I just wanted to wake up from this dream. I didn't want to have to stare down at the skeletons of my former owners. Here, they could no longer call me back from the garden for meals of roasted salmon and chicken. They could no longer cuddle and pet me when I felt down. They could no longer bring me wonderfully scented sprigs of catnip from the garden and throw dry treats to me out of a foil-lined bag. None of this seemed to exist now.

No, this couldn't come to pass.

"Get me out of here," I said. *"Please, I can't take this..."*

"Then take responsibility," the crystal said. *"And do what you have to do."*

The dream took me upwards, and the landscape beneath me faded to white. I found myself back inside my true mind once again, as the light intensified. Once it was bright enough, my eyes opened. I felt something pressing at my temples, almost as if it was trying to get in.

"Will you take your first gift?" the crystal's voice asked in my mind. *"Doing so will complete your union with your dragon, and you will be accepted as her rider."*

I took a deep breath, then looked back to Salanraja, who had one of her massive eyebrows raised. I guess I didn't have much of a choice in the matter. If I didn't do it, she'd probably eat me alive.

If I did though, she would probably feed me and look after me, just like my owners did in South Wales. But I was sure she'd make me have to work for that food. My previous owners would just dish it out into my bowls, on schedule three times a day.

"I accept," I said. *"Though, I wish you would at least tell me what this gift was."*

"You shall learn soon enough. Now, open your mind."

"How—" I didn't have a chance to finish my question, because a sudden pain seared into my temples at both sides as if someone had suddenly thrust a huge iron spike through my head. It came so quickly

that I didn't have time to yelp out. I only could grimace, and then the pain was gone.

Presently, the light from the crystal got brighter again, until it burned as intensely as a sun. But I couldn't close my eyes against it. It felt as if my lids had been glued to my brows, and the magic from the crystal bored right through my skull.

At the same time, I felt something leaving me. It floated out of my chest, where a faint and very thin blue thread of light emerged. A similar effect came from Salanraja – both threads connecting right to the centre of the crystal, which started spinning on its own axis.

More visions flashed through my mind's eye. I saw my past – the glorious bowls of food, resting on the sofa as my owners petted me, fighting other cats out of my territory, chasing squirrels along the garden fence, and then leaping into the hawthorn to scare away a sparrow. Then, I saw my future. Although, I should say, I saw many possible threads of my future. One had me dying through hunger due to days of roaming, looking for food that didn't exist on the dusty earth. Another had one of those bat-buzzard creatures slashing me off a dragon's back. In others, I was confident and powerful – swiping gems out of golems' eyes, or I commanded a dragon over a battlefield, armoured soldiers lined up like matchstick men below as I battled against a warlock, a blue beam of energy from my staff meeting head on with a red bolt of energy from his.

The visions flashed faster and faster through my mind until I saw nothing but a fluid and constant blur. A buzzing sound emerged in my ears, so loud it was painful. The sound intensified, increasing in pitch as if building to a climax.

All the time, the light got stronger and stronger in front of my eyes, and it seemed to emit an intense heat, as if I was sitting there cooking under Salanraja's flame. Whiskers, for all I knew, this might be her way of eating me. Using the crystal to hypnotise me like a frog in water slowly coming to the boil.

Either I was in the afterlife, or I'd survived, because all of a sudden, the images, the heat, and the terrible buzzing vanished. I opened my eyes to stare right into the facets of the crystal. But they were now a dull grey, slightly yellowed by the light from the sun.

"Is that it?" I asked Salanraja. *"I thought I was meant to get a gift?"*

I felt strangely empty not having the crystal's voice in my head anymore. It felt like those times my owners had gone on holiday and left me to stew with the other cats in the cattery. I could never understand the moggies you met there, and they didn't seem to understand me either. Many of them had lost their grace, their pride for the hunt, their sense of uniqueness, their wild side. They just seemed to want to sleep all day, and many of them didn't even care so much about food.

They'd become fully domesticated. They'd forgotten who they were – descendants of the great beasts of the plains, the jungles, the mountains, the forests. It was as if their ancestry had leached out of their very bones.

Salanraja lowered her head to me and studied me beneath her thick eyebrows. *"You are different,"* she said. *"I can see it in your eyes."*

"What? How?" I examined my paws, extending my paws and then my claws, looking for even a minor alteration. Then, I craned my neck and licked the fur on my side, wondering if I tasted any different. Everything was exactly the same.

Salanraja opened her mouth, and I darted out of the way, thinking she was about to breathe fire on me. Maybe she thought my new superpower was invulnerability. Instead, she spoke out loud in a remarkably clear and deep voice. "You can understand me now, can you not?"

I looked up at her with wide eyes. "You speak cat?" I said, and I thought I said it in my own language.

"No, I speak the dragon tongue," she replied. "Now, it appears you do too."

"What's the point of doing that when I can talk to you in my head?" I had the sinking feeling of being cheated. All those promises of being able to shoot fire out of staffs and cast intense beams of energy at warlocks. Now, this crystal had given me an ability that I already had.

"I also prefer to communicate with you that way," Salanraja said, still out loud. "It will help preserve my voice for when I need it the most."

I growled at her. "You didn't answer my question."

Salanraja let off a deep and loud sigh. She continued to speak, as we had been previously, inside my mind. *"I will tell you what abilities you've gained, because you seem too ignorant to work it out yourself. Firstly, now we're bonded we can communicate like this across vast distances. But it's not just me you can speak with, but any sentient creature. The crystals have gifted you with the magic of language. Do you realise how powerful that can be?"*

I yawned, and I turned away from the dragon. *"I still think it's pretty lame."*

"I'm sure you'll find good uses for it," Salanraja replied.

"I wonder how long that will take."

"That is surely up to you. Now hop on, it's time to return to Dragonsbond Academy."

I mewled, remembering the venison Salanraja had promised me. After everything that had happened, admittedly, I was famished. Salanraja turned her tail towards me, and I ran up it into the corridor on her back. She took off into the cerulean sky, and then she swooped down again to pick up the crystal with her talons.

"One more thing," she said. *"We must now defend this crystal at all costs. It is now the medium of our bond."*

"And what does that mean?"

"It means that if anyone destroys it, then both of us shall die."

10

KINSHIP

My mouth was watering by the time the castle, or Dragonsbond Academy as Salanraja styled it, came into sight. I couldn't imagine anything but that wonderful tender venison that she'd promised me.

I'd been pretty sleepy on the way through, and I'd drifted in and out of dreamland several times. Fortunately, Salanraja had kept her flight gentle. She was probably tired too, after everything. This made the corridor of Salanraja's spikes feel like a cradle that could rock me gently to sleep. My dreams were sweet, of venison and the gamey and majestic taste of it.

Soon enough, I woke up to see the castle getting ever bigger, and the tower containing Salanraja's chamber speeding towards us. She touched down with a soft thud, and I lifted myself up and stretched and yawned. I looked down Salanraja's corridor of spikes towards the shiny castle floor.

Guess what? There was no venison there, and the floor had a polished look, as if someone had just swept and scoured it clean.

I shrieked out loud, and I tried to tear my claws into Salanraja's flesh. But her skin was still tough, and it probably hurt me more than it hurt her. Before she could retaliate, I ran down her back and off her tail. I turned to the dragon.

"*There's no venison,*" I said. "*Salanraja, you promised.*"

Salanraja glanced over at the spot where the carcass had been. She then turned to me and gave a devilishly wicked grin. "*So there isn't,*" she said. "*They must have given it to another dragon. We can't have meat going off in this place. It will attract crows.*"

I felt the rage burning in my chest. "*Eaten by another dragon? That was my venison, Salanraja. You promised it to me.*"

"*I did nothing of the sort,*" Salanraja replied, shaking her head slowly. "*I only said that I might let you have some of it, which you did. You can't claim someone else's hunt as your own. What are you, a scavenger?*"

"*A scavenger?*" I took a step forward and then arched my back to make myself seem as big as possible.

"*Well, isn't that what you do? You eat the food that others have hunted and farmed after all.*"

"*That doesn't make me a scavenger... How could you call me such a thing?*"

"*You're the one accusing me of breaking promises. If there's one thing you should know about dragons is that we always keep our word. It's our code, and it keeps us noble.*"

But I wasn't listening to her nonsense. "*You promised me venison, and you lied to me. For that, I shall make you pay!*" I turned around, strolled back up to the corner, and then I angled my behind towards the wall and sprayed there.

Salanraja let out a deep threatening growl, and smoke rose from her flared nostrils. "*What in the Seventh Dimension do you think you're doing?*" she asked.

"*That should teach you,*" I replied. "*This is my territory now, and any food that enters it I claim as my own.*"

"*You just urinated in my home!*"

"*But it's mine now. I've just marked it so.*"

"*What are you talking about?*"

I lowered my back and scowled up at the dragon. "*Don't you know how to mark territory?*"

"What do you mean, territory?"

"Have you forgotten what it's like to be wild? Pah, you're just like the moggies in the cattery."

"You're insane. Now get out the way, before that stuff you've just put there starts to stink."

"I'm not moving," I said, and I lowered my front to the ground and growled, ready to mark the wall again.

"Move, or you shall burn!"

Salanraja lifted her neck, and her glands started to swell there. More smoke seeped out of her nostrils, like steam does a kettle. Then, she pulled back her head, and a jet of flame leaped out towards me.

I darted just out of the way in time, and I turned to the dragon, screeching and hissing out swear words in my own language. *"You could have killed me!"*

"Oh, you're nimble, you would have got out of the way in time. Now, never do that again, because I hate having to clean up after smelly creatures."

I wanted to give her some more of my mind. But before I could even put word to thought, a scratchy voice coming from the doorway interrupted me. It belonged to an old man.

"What in the Seventh Dimension is going on here?" he said.

11

MEETING THE ALCHEMIST

T he old man was huddled over a staff with a blue crystal on top of it, polished and ground into a smooth bevel at the edges. I actually couldn't tell how old he was. He had a multitude of wrinkles set deep into his skin, but he didn't look sallow or pale, as a lot of incredibly old humans might. Rather, he emanated a sense of vitality – not only through the colour of his skin but also out of his brilliant blue eyes.

Salanraja turned to him. The way both the old man and the dragon looked at each other, told me they were talking telepathically. I felt a little jealous, admittedly, to have Salanraja talking to someone in my own presence, without having a clue what they were saying. I mewled, trying to get some attention, but that didn't distract either of them. So, I looked at the scorched stone where I had sprayed and considered remarking it. But I thought better of the idea and instead put my nose to the floor and tried to sniff out a scrap of venison that whoever had cleaned this place might have overlooked.

Eventually, the old man hobbled over to me on his staff. He stooped over it and put down his hand to pet me. His skin was dry and wrinkled but he didn't seem scary in any way. I rubbed my face against his hand, then looked up to him and mewled again, thinking he might have food.

I let him tickle me underneath my chin, as I tried to find out what he and Salanraja had been talking about.

"Can you talk to anyone like that?" I asked Salanraja.

"Like what?"

"Like you do with me, in my head."

"Not now I'm bonded to you," Salanraja said. *"Now you're the only non-dragon I can connect to telepathically."*

"Then how did you just speak to him? And don't try to tell me you were just staring at each other like lovers."

"I talked through his dragon. He's a dragon rider too, you know."

"Oh," I said.

Meanwhile, the old man had now started to scratch behind my ear. It tickled a little, so I gently pushed away his hand with my paw. The old man smiled.

"We can talk, you know, Bengie?" he said. "The crystals gave you that gift."

"Not Bengie," I said. "Bengie is an awful name. Call me Ben."

The old man turned to Salanraja, and she chuckled from deep in her belly. *"Bengie is a much better name, so much more elegant,"* she said to me.

"It's a childish name," I said.

"Ben sounds like a commoner."

"Better that than what a child might name a stuffed toy."

I mewled at the old man again, jealous of the attention he was giving Salanraja. He turned back to me.

"Salanraja refuses to use the name I prefer," I said. "But you seem to have much more respect…" I licked my paw, which had picked up a little of the taste of the venison from the floor.

"Very well," the old man said. "Ben it is. Meanwhile, I am Aleam. A dragon rider and also an alchemist and healer here at the academy. It's a pleasure to make the acquaintance of such a fascinating creature."

"The pleasure is all mine to be so fascinating," I said. "Now, do you have any food?"

The old man chuckled. "Yes. I heard Matron Canda complaining about the starving cat who tried to steal from her kitchens. That must have been you. You must be famished."

He reached into a leather pouch on his hip and produced out of it a chicken drumstick, yellowed with turmeric on the outside. I looked up at him, unable to distinguish between the rumbling sound in my tummy and my purr.

Aleam reached down and scratched me under the chin again, and then he threw the chicken on the floor. I picked it up in my mouth by the thigh bone and sequestered it over in the corner which I had marked. I ripped into the meat with my teeth, savouring a taste I hadn't experienced for months. The chicken was cold, admittedly. But it still tasted fresh, and slightly herby – the way I liked it.

"Well," Aleam said. "This is certainly going to rile up the Council of Three. They wanted to cut the spikes off Salanraja to make her saddleable again, but Salanraja wasn't having any of it."

I glanced over my shoulder at Aleam. "Yes, you humans have a habit of cutting off our body parts." The number of times they'd trimmed my claws, and there was something else their 'vet' had done to me when I was younger too – I won't go into that one.

"Thank you," Salanraja said to me. *"I'm glad to hear there's someone here who understands these things."*

Aleam shook his head. "I guess we do. If only they could hear you talk, maybe they'd think a little differently about cats. But for now, you're only here to catch mice. Except for Ta'ra, that is. But many don't believe Ta'ra is actually a cat at all."

I finished the last scrap of meat off the chicken and then licked the remaining taste off my lips. So, it wasn't as good as venison, but chicken was still a great tasting classic.

I walked up to Aleam and rubbed my nose against his knee. He smelled like someone I could trust. I don't know how to describe it, really, but his scent had a certain cleanliness about it. Unlike Astravar, who smelled of dark things that set off thoughts of decay and despair in my mind, Aleam smelled of lavender perhaps, or like pollen drifting upon a warm summer breeze. It's these kinds of subtle things that tell a cat whether a human can be trusted from the start.

"Who's Ta'ra, anyway?" I asked. Where I came from, South Wales, the humans liked to say 'ta-ra' to people all the time. It meant goodbye.

"Ta'ra is quite a character, if I say so myself," Aleam replied. "But really, you should meet her for yourself. I think you two might get on well – if Ta'ra can get on with anyone, that is."

He turned on his heel and hobbled away on his staff. I turned around to Salanraja, who had already folded herself up on the floor. *"Go with Aleam,"* she said. *"I need a rest anyway, and I don't want you urinating all around this place while I sleep."*

I growled back at Salanraja. In all honesty, I didn't like her tone of voice. I turned back to Aleam and mewled again – kind of hoping he had more chicken.

"Come on, Ben," Aleam said. "Let's go and meet our friend."

He hobbled off, and I followed him into the corridors of this cold, unfriendly castle.

12

CAT SIDHE

I couldn't believe my eyes when I first saw Ta'ra. If it weren't for her size, she would have looked like a standard black cat, with a tapered face and wide round green eyes. But she was absolutely massive, and she didn't quite smell like a cat. Instead she had a wild scent about her. She sat propped up by a few cushions on a mahogany bench, licking her fur.

As soon as I entered Aleam's workshop, she stared at me and her eyes, I swear, started to glow. Her gaze had a kind of intensity that seemed able to measure the worth of my soul. But she didn't seem to think it worth very much at all, because she soon broke off her examination, yawned, and returned to grooming herself.

"Bengie, will you stop thinking so loud?" Salanraja said in my head. *"I'm trying to get some hard-earned sleep."*

"But she's ginormous," I said. *"She's even bigger than a Maine Coon."*

"Who?" Salanraja replied. *"And what in the Seventh Dimension is a Maine Coon?"*

"A Maine Coon is the biggest cat in the world. I thought everyone knew that." Although, to be honest, the Savannah cats often disagreed with that fact. They claimed that their grandfather was much, much bigger than the Maine Coon some of us saw on television. To which our old

neighbourhood Ragamuffin, perhaps the wisest of our clowder, pointed out that crossing a domestic cat with a serval of the Savannah to create a massive domestic cat is cheating. No domestic cat, he said, was bigger than the Maine Coon.

Salanraja laughed. *"I think you'll find the Sabre-Tooth tiger is the biggest cat in the world. Or, debatably, it might be the chimera."*

"Never heard of them."

"Well, if you don't quieten your thoughts a little, I might decide to drop you into a chimera's lair. Now, let me sleep."

I didn't know how I was meant to think quieter. But, although I didn't know what a chimera was, I honestly wasn't enthusiastic to find out either. I imagined myself whispering with each thought, and that seemed to do the trick. A moment later, something went quiet in my head, as if a voice nattering in there had shut itself off. Had that been Salanraja's thoughts?

The massive cat, Ta'ra, had now put her head down against a cushion and her eyes had sealed shut. Around her, a load of dusty looking books peered down from the high mounted bookshelves. The humans back in South Wales used to read much more glossy looking versions of these, but I'd never worked out what any of those funny symbols meant.

I wondered if I could also read the human language, now I could speak it. I tried to find a way up onto the shelves, but I couldn't see one. So instead, I sauntered over to see what Aleam was up to.

He stood over a complex glass alembic – and I wouldn't have known the word for that if the crystal hadn't granted me the gift of language. It was a collection of tubes and bulbs with green and yellow liquids bubbling within. Aleam peered over, studying the apparatus through a pair of glasses he had balanced on the bridge of his nose. After a while, he nodded as if in satisfaction, raised his staff to the apparatus, said some words I didn't quite understand – even with my gift – and turned to face the bench.

"Ta'ra," he said. "You have a guest, and you haven't even said a word to him. Show some respect, for goodness' sake."

Ta'ra opened her eyes again, blinked slowly at me, and yawned once more. "He's a common house cat," she said, and I recognised her to be speaking in the human tongue.

I responded in my language, screaming out feline expletives that would have disgusted Aleam if he could understand them. "I'm no common cat," I told her in the same language. "I'm a Bengal. The greatest of all domesticated cats. A descendant of the great Asian leopard cat."

But the massive cat seemed nonplussed by this. "See what I mean. He speaks cat language. He should be out hunting mice and not bothering me here."

Aleam shook his head, and he opened his mouth as if he wanted to say something. But I decided it better to butt in and try to deflate this cat's ego, which seemed almost as large as its bulk.

"What in the whiskers are you?" I said in the human language. "You look like a cat, but you don't look like a cat."

Ta'ra snarled at me. "I'm a much more spiritual creature than you can ever imagine. I can also look smaller, if it intimidates you less?" She stood up, and then for the first time I noticed her fur wasn't completely black. She had a single white diamond on her chest, neatly arranged as if someone had painted it there.

Then, the air seemed to shimmer around her, and she literally started to shrink in her chair. She went from being larger than a Maine Coon to the size of a normal cat within the space of seconds.

"What are you?" I asked again.

The cat let out a loud, desultory laugh. "If you were as intelligent as you like to think, you would know. Those versed in the ways of magic would call me a Cat Sidhe. I'm of the Faerie Realm, once a princess, but fate changed my form. You don't have a clue what I'm talking about, do you?"

I tried to blink off my disbelief. I must have been dreaming; this couldn't have been real.

"Ta'ra," Aleam said. "Don't be so judgemental. Ben is not of this world. Astravar teleported him here from another dimension, and he would still be under the warlock's thrall now if he hadn't managed to escape."

"Judgemental? I'm the most misunderstood fae of them all. Don't you think I have a right to be judgemental sometimes?" The black cat stood up, slinked off the bench, and then she walked up to examine me.

"So, tell me, Ben… How did you come to speak the human tongue, and why did you end up under the service of someone as foul as Astravar?"

"He brought me here," I said. "I was eating the best dinner of salmon trimmings I'd tasted in a long time, and I was just about to lap up some milk, when I got flung out of his portal right on to his hard stone floor." I thought being a cat, Ta'ra might understand what a travesty it was to be suddenly separated from a good meal.

She stared at me, blinking. I might have known she wouldn't quite get it.

"Why aren't you in the cattery like the rest of the cats?" I asked. "Don't you get along with them?"

"Because I'm not a cat, I'm a fae," she snapped back. "Once a fairy with a 'y', until I got banished from the kingdom because of my new form."

"A what?"

She growled from deep inside her stomach. "Do you really know so little about the magical worlds?"

"I didn't even know magic existed until I met Astravar."

Ta'ra shook her head like a human would. "And I didn't know that cats existed either until Astravar summoned me away from my wedding ceremony to Prince Ta'lon and decided that he would change my life completely. Gone were my wings, replaced by this furry body and my claws. It was horrible."

"So, you don't enjoy being a cat?" Such a notion seemed utterly unfathomable to me.

Ta'ra looked over at the bubbling solution. "Astravar gave me the ability to turn back into a fairy eight times. I've used up six of them, three because of my own stupidity. Aleam has been trying all this time to find a cure for my curse, but I fear that only the curser can reverse it. I can transform twice more, only for a day mind, then I'll be stuck with this terrible form for life."

"Terrible?" I really couldn't understand this lady. "Cats are the greatest creatures alive."

"No, you're not," Ta'ra said. "You just think you are. But you don't have wings, you don't have magic, and you can't even look after yourselves. Cat-hood is the pinnacle of reliance, and none of you seem to understand how demeaning it is." She examined her paw.

I was starting to feel attacked. I arched my back and circled around Ta'ra, baring my teeth as I did so. She did the same, looking at me with those bright green eyes.

"We can hunt," I said.

"Can you? I've heard of cats who tried to run away from Dragonsbond Academy. They didn't last two days out there, before they came back to the kitchens mewling for food."

I felt the hackles rise on my back. "They're merely useless moggies. But I'm different, I'm a Bengal, a descendent of the great Asian leopard cat. And I can hunt. In fact, I killed thousands of mice for Astravar."

"Ooh, big deal. You reached into a hole and scooped out defenceless mice with nowhere to go but their holes. There's a difference to catching mice in a human dwelling and hunting in the wild. My instincts tell me you wouldn't be very good at the latter."

"Oh yeah," I said. "I'll show you what a wild cat I am."

I lunged forward at Ta'ra, scratching with my claw. I hit her on her shoulder, and she responded with a loud shrieking sound as she batted back with her claws. Then, she grew in size until she was almost as big as a human child. I didn't let that scare me, and I clawed at her leg, a primal part of me wanting to do much damage.

How dare she imply I was a poor hunter. How dare she imply I was useless.

Ta'ra continued to grow until she was towering above me, and then she pinned me underneath her massive paws. I tried to scratch her off me, but she kept me pinned, with a wicked grin on her face. "I'm a witch, you know. That's what they call me, a witch!"

Aleam had been so busy with his experiment, that he'd been completely oblivious to what was going on. But I guess the two of us screeching so loudly caused him to turn his attention towards us.

"What, in the Seventh Dimension?" he said, and he quickly hobbled over on his staff. He used it to take a swipe at Ta'ra. She batted at it and then clutched onto it with one paw while she kept me pinned down with the other.

"Ta'ra," Aleam said. "Let go at once."

Ta'ra hissed at him, but Aleam glared back with his cold blue eyes. Ta'ra had the bottom of the staff in her grasp, and the top of it glowed bright yellow.

"He started it," Ta'ra said.

Aleam turned to me, and a stern look stretched across his eyebrows. "Is this true, Ben?"

I snarled at Ta'ra. "She provoked me," I said.

Aleam turned on Ta'ra. "What have I told you about your moods? You really have to work on this."

The angry green glow in Ta'ra's eyes faded, and soon enough she let go of the staff and let off an apologetic meow. She lifted her paw from me, and I immediately wriggled free, hissing at the cat. But she looked at me, an abashed, guilty look in her wide eyes, as if she'd just stolen chicken off of a human's dinner table.

"I'm sorry, Ben," she said. "It's just... Astravar did this to me. Sometimes, my emotions... I just hate it!"

"We will find a cure, eventually." Aleam took hold of a cloth on the table, and he began to polish his crystal that had now stopped glowing. "We may not be able to turn you back to a normal fairy, but I think we'll find a way to stop the episodes."

Ta'ra meowed again, and she then shrunk back down to normal cat size and slinked back over to the bench and leapt back onto it. She was soon yawning, and then she closed her eyes and was quickly fast asleep.

I heard footsteps, and I smelled a human approaching the door. I darted under the table and hid behind the leg, remembering how that woman had treated me in the kitchen. But it wasn't the chef who arrived there, but a spotty faced teenager, no older than sixteen, with a scroll in his hand. He had a short sword in a sheath hanging off his hip, and a staff with a blue crystal head fastened to the back.

"Driar Aleam," he said. "I'm sorry to disturb your work, but I'm looking for a moggie. Apparently one with unusual leopard like spots. Have you seen him anywhere?"

"He's right here," Aleam pointed down to where I was crouched, trying to make myself as small as possible. "Ben, don't be shy. Why don't you come out and say hello to your dragon rider peer?"

I mustered up a little courage, and I moved out from under the table. The dragon rider boy had blond hair, and a hard jaw behind his spots. When they eventually cleared away, humans would probably see him as handsome.

The boy looked down at me, contempt evident in his eyes.

"Well, Ben, this is Initiate Rine," Aleam said.

I opened my mouth to say something, but the boy scoffed and then turned on his heel. He glanced back at me over his shoulder. "Come on, you'll be late. You really don't want to keep the council waiting."

He marched off, leaving me no option but to follow on his heels. As he walked, I could swear I heard him mutter under his breath, that he couldn't believe I was a 'bleeding cat'.

13

THE COUNCIL OF THREE

The dragon rider boy led me to a courtyard, and he walked so fast, it was hard even for a cat to keep up. He had quite a stride about him, as if he regarded himself in a higher station than he actually was. Meanwhile, he didn't turn his head to look at me even once.

We walked past the kitchens, and I could smell bread baking in there. I was half tempted at one point to abandon this Initiate Rine character and instead give the woman who had attacked me earlier with a spoon – who I think Aleam had called Matron Canda – a piece of my mind. She would be surprised to have a cat talking to her, for sure. Maybe it would even scare her away for a while, leaving me alone to enjoy some food.

But despite the hunger still rumbling in my tummy, I continued onwards. I hadn't heard from Salanraja yet, and I wondered if she'd end up joining us in this special meeting.

"What does this Council want with me?" I tried asking Initiate Rine. But my question didn't seem to warrant an answer from him. Rather, he just sped up.

He dashed through the corridors, and we passed a group of young adults making a racket and laughing as they moved forward in a crowd. I had to concentrate to stop myself getting trampled as I weaved my way between their legs. Really, half of them didn't even seem to notice I was there.

Soon, we found ourselves inside the bailey of the castle which was surrounded by tall crenelated castle walls. Those walls looked fun to climb, and I imagined myself running along them chasing birds and butterflies. But then all I saw flying around here were dragons and crows, and I didn't fancy chasing either of those. We reached an archway in the wall that led into an inner courtyard.

"In here," Initiate Rine said, and he gestured with his short sword. "I shall wait outside."

Alone, I entered a cloistered section of the castle, surrounded by an outside corridor raised up by columns. Doors led into the castle, but most of these were closed. A neatly mown patch of lawn covered the centre of the courtyard, cut off by a raised semi-circular platform built from a chequered pattern of rough red and white stones.

Four pillars led up from this platform, supporting a domed roof. Underneath this stood two women and a man behind three wooden lecterns. Each had short swords sheathed on their hips, staffs hanging from their backs, and mustard coloured shoulder pads, with golden thread woven through them in an ornate floral pattern. They were all old, and I could see that without even needing to be close to them. The gems in their staffs were red, blue, and green respectively.

I approached them slowly at first, wondering which of them posed the greatest threat. I'd seen the dragon riders use their staffs from their dragons, and right now I didn't doubt that one of them might have wanted to scorch me alive. They all wore these white robes, secured with cords that hung down above the floor. Something about the way they frowned at me told me they weren't really on my side.

The first of the women, the one on my left, had the red staff and her grey hair was swept back and tied in a bun. She also had wrinkles at the corners of her eyes so deep, they looked like fruit flies could use them for flight training. She was as thin as a scarecrow, with long arms and legs that almost looked as if they didn't fit her body.

"I am Driar Yila," she called out to me. "Approach, cat."

As I got even closer, the second woman opened her mouth to

speak. "We are the Council of Three," she said. "And I am Driar Lonamm." She was a little plumper than the first – meaning she probably liked food and that we had something in common. Though her face also displayed many wrinkles, her fiery wavy red hair made her look a little younger.

The third elder was a good two feet taller than the women, a giant by any measure. He had a bald head, a pockmarked face, and thick corded hands that made me think his bulk was largely muscle.

"My name is Driar Brigel," he said. "And it is time to test your worth."

Once I got close enough, I noticed a white crystal hanging from rafters on the underside of the dome. The three elders lifted their staffs off of their backs and pointed them at the crystal. Beams of their respective colours shot out of the staffs, and they soon merged to infuse the crystal with a powerful light.

It glowed brightly, bathing the courtyard with a blinding light. Whiskers, it seemed almost as bright as the sun. But soon, the light faded a little to display an image. It showed a view of my own crystal, with my dreams once again running through it – me on Salanraja's back with a staff clasped firmly in my jaw, as I shot fireballs out of it into those massive bat-like creatures.

But that wasn't all the crystal showed. It also showed the inside of Salanraja's chamber, with the dragon sleeping on the polished stone floor, her massive eyelids clasped so tightly shut that it didn't look like she'd be waking soon. Her nostrils flared as her lips vibrated, as if letting out huge snores. Plumes of smoke rose out of her nose, and drifted over towards my crystal, almost as if it was sucking them in.

"There she is, sleeping during important affairs," the thin elder, Driar Yila said.

"Typical Salanraja," the male, Driar Brigel said. "When is she going to learn?"

"I thought she'd soon let us make her saddleable," Driar Lonamm said with a slow shake of the head. "Then she pulls this stunt."

Driar Yila turned a hard stare on to me. "And now here is the specimen she chose as a rider. Not a human, or a dwarf, or even a lowly troll. No, he's your run-of-the-mill cat!"

When I heard them speak about me this way, I couldn't help but arch up my back and hiss at Driar Yila. But she didn't even blink, her stare seeming to bore right into my soul. The other two elders, whose gazes had drifted up towards the crystal, also turned their heads back towards me and met my gaze with equally probing stares.

"I'm not just a cat," I said. "I'm a Bengal, a descendant of the Asian leopard cat."

A smile crept across Driar Brigel's lips. "Ah, so the rumour is true. You can speak our language. But we still don't understand why the dragon chose you."

"Driar Brigel," Driar Yila said without taking her eyes off me, "we shouldn't be having this conversation without the dragon. Wake her up, cat. I presume you can at least do that."

"What? You want me to just run over there and stamp on her head? She won't be happy."

Driar Yila raised an eyebrow. "I thought you were bonded?"

"We are, but—"

"Then you should be able to wake her from here."

"I…"

Driar Yila opened her mouth to say something more, but Driar Lonamm raised a hand to stop her. "We can't just expect a cat to know what humans do. He's not had the same education as us, and he has a much smaller brain. Cat—"

"I have a name," I cut in.

Lonamm froze and she gave me a stern look. She twisted her staff, and I waited for her to throw some magic at me. But after a moment she said, "so tell me that name."

"Ben," I said.

She smirked. "Very well, Ben. Talk to your dragon loud enough, and she'll wake."

"Are you crazy? She'll break my bones first, and then she'll eat you alive."

"She won't," Driar Yila snapped back. "Now do it!"

"As you wish," I said. "It's your funeral." Just as I'd imagined myself whispering before, now I imagined myself screeching as if I'd just landed in the same garden as an unfamiliar dog. To put some extra flare into it, I arched my back and let the hackles shoot up. Then, I felt Salanraja wake, and she wasn't happy.

A loud roar resounded out from one of the towers behind me. In the crystal above, I saw her rise on her two hind legs, charge out into the sky, and then she screamed in my mind.

❦ 14 ❧

A MISSION

"I warned you not to wake me, or you'd find yourself in a chimera's lair," Salanraja said. She was certainly angry.

"I had no choice," I replied.

"What do you mean you had no choice?"

"The Council of Three," I said. "A spotty faced boy came to look for me, and then he told me to go and see them. These people, they're so rude. They think they're the greatest things that ever lived."

I felt Salanraja calm down a little. It was as if the same dragonfire burning within her also burned within my chest. "Humans. They will always be arrogant. But they are in charge here."

I couldn't help but laugh, at least inside my mind. I didn't want to end up fried by the magic that these elders were spewing out of their staffs. "I thought you said dragons were the most powerful creatures to have ever lived, and yet you are subject to humans."

"They don't control us," Salanraja said. A shadow passed overhead and a moment later, Salanraja thudded onto the ground, shaking the earth a little.

I looked at her, unimpressed, and yawned. "If they don't control you, why are they waking you up?"

Salanraja lowered her neck to me and examined me with those

massive yellow eyes. *"They are bonded to their dragons, remember? All Dragon riders are. Their dragons are part of the Council too, and right now the humans will be communicating with their dragons to work out what to do next. So, I'm not answering to them, but their dragons."*

"So why aren't the dragons here too?"

"The Council deemed it would be less intimidating to have massive dragons looming over potential Initiates."

"I see. Also, what's a Driar?" I asked. I had so many questions.

Salanraja examined one of her claws, extending it slightly. *"A Driar is a dragon rider who has graduated from Dragonsbond Academy. Either they work at King Garmin's castle, or they are stationed here as teachers or lookouts."*

She then turned to the council, and I felt the rage flare in her chest again. She opened her jaws wide, displaying those tremendously long teeth, and she let out a loud roar. I could swear that she was about to breathe fire on the elders and roast them there and then. Well, they couldn't say I didn't warn them.

The three elders examined her for a moment. They raised their staffs, and the crystal above us flashed bright white.

"Calm yourself, Salanraja," Driar Yila shouted. "That is a command."

Salanraja continued to rage. She gnashed and clawed at nothing in particular. Really, she looked as if she'd caught rabies, and I half expected her to start foaming at the mouth.

As she raged, the elders in front raised their staffs ever closer to the crystal above their heads, feeding it with more and more energy. The intensity inside brightened so much that I thought it might explode.

Yila said something out loud. It was in a language I couldn't understand at first, very similar in cadence to what I'd heard Aleam speaking before in his study. I would have thought that I could understand all languages because of the crystal's gift. But then, I guessed they were speaking in the language of the crystals, and crystals weren't technically creatures.

Suddenly, everything went quiet. It was as if someone had just smashed a wineglass at a party, and everyone was looking around wondering who broke it. Salanraja let out a whimper, and she backed away. She buried her head in her front claws for a moment, almost as if she was crying. It took her awhile to emerge from that position.

"Salanraja," Driar Brigel said after a long moment, his muscles flexing underneath his robe. "I must say that we're disappointed. For a long time, we've tried to find you a suitable rider, and you only needed to trim your spikes to hold a saddle. But instead you go and choose this mangy creature as a rider. What were you thinking?"

Salanraja let out a low and quiet growl, but this soon turned into a soft whimper.

"*Aren't you going to say something to them?*" I asked.

"*I can't,*" Salanraja replied. "*I'm not bonded to them.*"

"*Then speak to their dragons.*"

"*I'd rather not,*" Salanraja replied. "*They'll just remind me what a misfit they've always thought I am. This is an argument that I've never managed to win. Just tell the Driars that I think you are the most suitable candidate, and that you have as much strength of character as any human rider. And tell them that you're descended from a Sabre-Tooth tiger or something. Not one of those puny leopard cat things.*"

I did as she told me, leaving out the descendant from a Sabre-Tooth tiger part, as I'd already told them what I was descended from, and I saw absolutely no reason to mock my heritage.

"You never did quite get on with the other dragons," Brigel replied, directing his voice at Salanraja. "It won't hurt to cut off the spikes, you know. Once they've been gone a few days, you won't realise you ever had them."

"*No!*" Salanraja replied, and it took me a moment to realize that the shout only echoed in my head. Salanraja also let out another long roar. The elders reacted by lifting up their staffs towards the crystal again.

Salanraja corrected herself.

"*Look, stop getting all angry all the time,*" I said. "*I don't know about you, but I don't want to be on someone's plate for dinner.*"

"*I'm sorry,*" Salanraja said. "*But this is quite personal. This isn't just about my spikes. I can't have a human rider. I've never wanted one. I've never trusted any humans around here to want one as my rider. Apart from Aleam, but he's already bonded."*

"So, what do I tell them?" I asked.

"Tell them that you are ready to prove your worth. Tell them that we will serve honourably the Kingdom of Illumine, and the king, pompous as he is."

"Fine," I said. I turned back to the council and told them exactly what Salanraja had told me, not omitting a single detail. Yila scowled at the bit about the king being pompous and banged her staff loudly against the floor.

"I didn't ask you to say that part. Gracious demons, the Dragon Council will roast me alive if you're not careful."

"I said exactly what you asked me to."

"You, Bengie, it seems, have a lot to learn."

The elders at this point were conferring amongst themselves. While the two ladies continued to speak, Brigel turned back towards us. "Salanraja," he said. "Are you sure you want this? Despite your rebellious streak, we want to protect you. Having an incompetent dragon rider might cost you your life."

"But what's the alternative," I asked, and I didn't wait for Salanraja's permission to speak this time. "She's already bonded to me, isn't she?"

"They don't want us to unbond anymore," Salanraja explained. *"Now they want me to serve as a transport dragon for royal passengers and you as a regular rat-catcher. But I knew when I bonded with you that there was no turning back."*

"So, what do I tell them?"

"Tell them I've made up my mind."

I did just that, and Driar Lonamm sighed as she pivoted around back towards us. She examined Salanraja for a moment, then turned to me. "Well, I guess we'll have to learn to accept it at Dragonsbond Academy. Although for now we wish to keep this a secret from the palace. You'll need to prove your worth to us before news of your existence is published in the royal papers. Or, if you get yourselves killed, we could easily just cover this one up."

"What are you talking about?" I asked. "We're not going to die."

"Aren't you?" Driar Yila said. "You will eventually. No magic can stop fate."

"I will die when I'm old and have lived a good life," I said.

"So be it," Yila replied. She turned to Brigel, who nodded.

"Remind us of your name, again?" he said.

I stepped forward. "My name is Ben, because I'm Bengal, a descendant of the great Asian leopard cat."

Salanraja growled quietly. *Not that again.*

I hissed at her. Driar Brigel all this time, was watching our exchange with intent, as he leaned toward us. "Well, Ben," he said. "Do you promise to swear fealty to Dragonsbond Academy and the King of Illumine? Do you promise to serve as a loyal subject, and to put the fate of your kingdom before your own life? The truth now if you please."

Well, if he wanted the truth, I might as well give it. "I came from a pleasant house in South Wales where I could eat salmon every day. Here, I've eaten nothing in days except bugs, a tiny scrap of venison, and a bit of chicken. You want to know what I want? I want to go home."

I mewled as I spoke that last sentence, giving my best cat like cuteness that had won humans over so many times. I hoped that they'd know of some magic that could send me back through a portal across time and space. Tomorrow, I could be in South Wales, sleeping on the plush sofa in the conservatory, the sun coming through the windows. Later, I would chase birds and butterflies around the garden. I would feast every day like a cat should, and I would get food when I wanted it.

I was interrupted from my reveries by Driar Yila's staff banging against the floor. "You have no choice, you selfish creature," she said. "Either you do what we ask, or you'll spend the rest of your life chasing rats."

I hadn't expected that response. I mewled again, to try to get at least some of their sympathy for my plight, but they weren't having any of it. Eventually, I realised that this harsh mistress, Driar Yila, wouldn't bend one bit.

"Very well, I promise to serve your kingdom." But I also told myself I'd find a way to go home. There had to be some way back.

That grin returned to Brigel's face. Really, even though he was the bulkiest of the three, he also seemed the kindest. "Then, I think it's time to give you your first mission," he said. "Prove yourself at this, and we will accept the pairing into Dragonsbond Academy."

"What in the Seventh Dimension are they going to send us after now?" Salanraja said, and I mewled quietly, not liking the sound of danger. But I noticed the three elders were now looking at me, as if expecting me to say something.

"Go on," Salanraja said. *"Ask them what the mission is. Show some interest in helping out and things will be a little easier here."*

I looked at Salanraja, and she cocked her head towards the council. So, I turned back to them.

"What do you wish for us to do?" I asked, reluctantly.

Lonamm reached down into a hidden pocket at the front of her robe and pulled out a scroll. She fumbled with this a moment, struggling to open it with one hand, as she gripped her staff tightly in her other hand.

"Let me see," Lonamm said. "Yes, here it is. There's a bone dragon terrorising Midar Village on the edge of the Wastelands. Go there and stop it. Once you come back with proof that this has been done, then we will reconsider your application."

"Thank you," I said.

"That's not enough," Salanraja said. *"You need to bow."*

"I need to what?"

"Bow..."

"How the whiskers can a cat bow?"

"I don't know, just lower yourself on your front legs or something."

But I wasn't listening to this idiocy, and so I gave another meow instead. It wasn't so much to say thank you, but more to remind them that I still wanted to go home, and that if they could kindly open a portal back to the Brecon Beacons after this mission, I'd greatly appreciate it.

"Very well," Yila said, the harsh look not leaving her face. "Then be off with you, and remember, only return once the mission's complete."

"Fine," I said.

She glared at me as if expecting something.

"*You don't just say 'fine' here,*" Salanraja explained. "*You say, yes ma'am.*"

But I wasn't listening. I kept staring back at Driar Yila and then I yawned, licked my paw, and started grooming myself.

Driar Lonamm shook her head. "Go on, be off with you." She made a gesture as if shooing away a cat. But then, come to think of it, to them I was just that – a cat.

I slinked away, back towards the bailey. But before I could take a few steps, Salanraja gnashed her teeth loudly behind me, and made a sound like an angry dog.

"*Get on my back, you impudent fool,*" she said. "*Gracious demons, how did I end up choosing you?*"

I let out a deep growl, then I turned back to her. I really didn't feel like going anywhere after how these humans had treated me. But I guess we had a bone dragon to destroy. So, I ran up Salanraja's tail and secured myself in the corridor of spikes on her back.

As Salanraja lifted herself off the ground, I cursed at the three elders in cat language, safe in the knowledge that they (probably) wouldn't understand what I said.

15

MASTERY OF FLIGHT

I was getting the hang of flying. This was my third time in the air with Salanraja, and I was starting to enjoy the sensation of it. The sun beat down from the sky, bringing a pleasant warmth that offset the cool breeze. The clouds rolled by overhead, so far away they looked like massive balls of candy floss floating up in the sky. The yellow and green fields had been arranged so neatly beneath us that they reminded me of the board from that silly game that humans liked to play.

You must know which one I mean. The one where humans took it in turns – that sometimes could last for hours – to shuffle pieces around from one black or white chequered square to the next. The master and mistress of the bungalow back in winter used to love playing this in the winter besides the roaring log fireplace, the heat from it warming my soft fur. They would have salami and olives on the table, one which made me intensely hungry, and the other which made me just think, yeuch!

But honestly, this game was so boring that I would go over and sit on the master's lap and pretend to watch them for a while. Then, while he wasn't watching, I'd knock off the tallest of the pieces closest to me – the one that had the cross on it. The master would get so angry then, but the mistress would start laughing so loudly she'd spill her wine. Because she found it funny, I found it funny, so I continued to keep playing that way. Over time, the master would try to stop me getting anywhere near the pieces, blocking them off with his forearm, and so that became part of the game.

Of course, I always won.

As I watched the fields passing by beneath me, like a forever-moving floor, I purred from deep within my chest. I'd momentarily forgotten about those idiot humans back at Dragonsbond Academy. That was the beauty of being a cat. You didn't need to have any worries. You could just put everything behind you and focus on being in the moment.

But, at the same time, I could hear Salanraja growling and groaning from her chest somewhere beneath my feet. Occasionally she'd open her mouth, and out would emerge a ring of smoke that would drift off behind us, dissipating into the sky.

She was trying to get my attention, but I was having none of it. This was the first flight I was enjoying, even when my memories of home left a sinking feeling of wistfulness inside me.

Eventually, Salanraja must have realised she wasn't doing a great job of communicating her anger. So, she lurched to her side, and had me tumbling within her cage of spikes. My ribs made a nasty cracking sound as I bashed against the wall. Whiskers, that hurt.

"Ouch," I said. *"Fly in a straight line, will you?"*

"I'm sorry," she said, with a tinge of irony in her voice. *"But sometimes I need to turn."*

"Then turn gently. It's not as if we're navigating through a canyon."

"You don't get to tell me what to do," Salanraja said, and she did a few rolls in the air, sending me around and around again, like the proverbial cat in the washing machine.

I couldn't really focus on staying alive in there and talk to her at the same time. I thought I was going to throw up, and this time I'd do so on her back. But she stopped eventually, and the ground beneath my feet no longer looked like a chessboard, but rather was spinning around like a kaleidoscope.

"*What is wrong with you?*" I asked her.

"*What is wrong with me?*" She growled. "*It appears to be you who wants to get us killed. How could you behave so impudently in front of the Council of Three? Have you any idea how powerful they and their dragons are?*"

"I thought it was the warlocks who were the bad guys," I said. "Isn't the Council meant to be on your side?"

"*They are,*" Salanraja said, and paused. She beat her wings rapidly a few times to lift us up higher in the air and then lowered us into a glide. A large crow with a great grey beak soared alongside at the same level as us for a moment. But then, it noticed either Salanraja or me, and probably her. It cawed out and then dived back down towards the ground.

"*They are,*" Salanraja said again, "*and you're right, they probably would never kill us. It's just...*"

"What?" I said gently, thinking better to keep her calm than to aggravate her back into stunt mode.

Salanraja shook her head slowly, causing her body to sway slightly underfoot. "*Dragons aren't usually born with spikes like these on our backs. Usually we have horns that come out of our heads, and sometimes a line of spikes along our spine. The other dragons call me Double Ribs, and they ask me what I'm keeping inside my cage. Some dragons understand why I don't want to change myself, but others feel I should just get rid of these spikes.*"

"*So why don't you?*" I asked.

"*Would you ever want to get rid of your claws and your teeth? These things are a part of me now. I was born with them, and I've learned to fly with them. They make me strong, and I can even use them to knock other dragons out of the sky. It's an extra defence mechanism.*"

I turned my head to the side. The crow had come back up to join us now, albeit at a much more cautious distance. Its black eye watched me, as if trying to assess if I was friend or foe. I lost interest in it and turned to look at the horizon, appreciating the cool wind swishing through my fur.

"*Isn't there like a human who could ride you without a saddle?*" I asked. "*A small lady, perhaps, who would be happy to lie in this 'ribcage'?*"

Salanraja groaned. "*You would never find any human willing to ride a* dragon without a saddle, and even if you did, the elders would never allow it."

"Why not?"

"Because they're human, and they're all about keeping safe. That's what this war against the warlocks is about for King Garmin, creating a world that is safe."

"And they don't care about my safety?" I asked, remembering what Driar Yila had said about covering up my death.

"I guess not," Salanraja replied. "You're just a cat to them. Which makes you expendable."

Salanraja flapped her wings a few times, gently this time. The crow was still there, and it was now edging a little closer to us. But Salanraja paid it no heed. The sun hid behind a cloud, and the world went darker for a moment.

That was when I noticed a thin purple line emerging from the horizon.

"There it is," Salanraja said. "The Wastelands."

I licked my paw. "What are the Wastelands, anyway?"

"No man's land," Salanraja replied. "A land full of magical creatures, some of them serving the King's mages, while others are machinations of the warlocks. It's a vast battlefield that separates the Kingdom of Illumine from the Darklands where the Warlocks reside. You must have passed through them when you came to Illumine, as Astravar's tower is right on the edge of them."

I remembered that yucky boggy land that I'd sprinted through before reaching Illumine. Though I hadn't seen any magical creatures in there, I had contended with that suffocating purple gas.

My tummy rumbled. "Can we stop for a bite to eat before we get there," I asked. "They mentioned a village. Perhaps they might have a kitchen and a chef willing to at least donate a fish or two."

Salanraja laughed. "Do you ever think about anything else?" she asked. "It's like everything I've heard from you since I met you has been food, food, food, food, food..."

"That's because I've not eaten for days," I said.

"What about that chicken Aleam gave you?"

"*It was one drumstick. Do you really think one drumstick is enough to feed a busy Bengal?*"

"*Busy?*"

"*Yes, you've made me busy. My life before I came to this place was eat, groom, sleep, play. Now, we're off chasing a bone dragon through some disgusting lands which I really wanted to see the back of.*"

"*Oh, quit moaning,*" Salanraja said. "*I tell you what. When this is all over, I'll hunt you something nice, and we can feast together.*"

"*Like that venison you promised?*"

Salanraja let out a plume of smoke. "*Venison if you like. Or pheasant, or a nice roasted mutton.*"

"*How about salmon?*" I asked.

"*No, we're not going fishing. It's got to be real hunting.*"

"*Fine,*" I said. "*Just make sure you stick to your promise this time, or you'll be sorry.*"

I had been so curious about this strange world I'd been thrust into that I hadn't even realised how much greyer the ground beneath had become. The sky was truly darkening around us, and a purple haze floated over the ground below. I looked down at it, truly not wanting to go back to that land. I really didn't want to have to meet Astravar again, whether I had a dragon or not.

"*Just one more question,*" I said. "*What's so special about warlocks, anyway? How are they any different from the king's mages?*"

"*It's to do with the crystals they use,*" Salanraja replied. "*Warlocks use dark crystals; mages use light crystals.*"

"*So, there are only two types of crystals.*"

"*Yes,*" Salanraja said. "*Something like that. Dark crystals drain life and draw off its power, while the magic of white crystals focuses on creation. Mages can readily use white magic, but dark magic is now banned in Illumine after how it completely corrupted the minds of the warlocks. That's the thing about dark magic – you use too much of it and it darkens your soul.*"

"*Then what about the dragon riders,*" I asked. "*What kind of magic do we use?*"

"*Really, dragon riders and dragons use a mixture of light and dark through a very special kind of crystal. It's the bond between dragons and their human riders that stops dark magic corrupting us. In most cases, anyway."*

"You mean there are dark dragon riders?"

Salanraja lowered her head, and I felt a tinge of sadness in her soul. *"Out there somewhere,"* she said, *"yes, there are. But they are a story for another day, because it looks like we've arrived."*

Now the land beneath us smelled intensely familiar. I don't know how to describe the sensation. It wasn't a physical smell, as such, but rather one that emerged in the mind. It reminded me of memories rooted in my primal ancestry. The fear of not being at the top of the food chain, knowing there were things in the sky that might swoop down and lift you up in their claws and tear your flesh away from the bone. The fear of great lizards roaming the land on two legs. The fear of death, and the fear of living forever alone. This fear smelt like death and decay and all the rotten things of the soul.

The purple mist was thick below us now, seeping all over the ground. It wove its way through the red reeds sticking out of the swamps. This wasn't a place for cats. In fact, it wasn't a place for any living creatures. No wonder I'd found it so hard to find food here.

"There," Salanraja said. *"Do you see it?"*

"Do I see what?"

"Our quarry... The bone dragon."

I lifted myself up onto my front paws and I climbed up to the top of Salanraja's external ribcage and peered out from between the spikes. Then I saw it, streaking across the sky. A great skeletal beast, long and terrifying, similar to what the crystal had shown me.

The creature veered towards us, and then it tossed its head up to the sky and roared.

16

BEDSHEET OF LIGHT

Salanraja was gliding closer and closer to the ground. She didn't seem to want to lift herself up again, perhaps worried that the bone dragon might hear her if she flapped her wings even once. Or perhaps she had decided that we weren't going to fight the bone dragon at all, that instead we would hide in a swamp until it flew away, Salanraja submerged like a crocodile. I have to admit, I preferred that latter solution.

"*That's no normal bone dragon,*" Salanraja said. "*I wish the council had told me we were dealing with one of those.*"

"*One of what?*" I asked.

"*Shh!*" Salanraja whispered. "*Don't make a sound. Not even a purr.*"

"*What is it? What's so dangerous about that thing?*"

"*Are you telling me you'd be happy to meet this thing on a dark night and a new moon? Would you invite it to a party?*"

"*You're a dragon, and it's made of bone. Just throw some flame at it and burn it out of the sky.*"

Salanraja turned back to me and looked at me with one eye. "*You really think you're smart, don't you? You've got it all figured out. As long as the Manipulator is there on the ground, then its summoned creature can't die.*"

"*A what?*"

"*A Manipulator.*" Salanraja landed softly on the ground, kicking up some dust that glistened purple in the waning light. "*It should be around here somewhere. You've got sharp eyes haven't you, Bengie? Look for a change in patterns. A shimmer in the air.*"

I tried to peer through the murk, but I could see nothing. "*I don't think there's anything even there,*" I said, "*and I don't believe in ghosts.*"

Salanraja scoffed. "*It's not a ghost, it's a Manipulator, as I said.*"

"*But you haven't even told me what a Manipulator is.*"

"*It's a warlock's conjuration that allows him to cast spells from a safe position. Anything under the Manipulators' control is invulnerable until you kill the Manipulator. Gracious demons, can't you smell the thing?*"

"*No, I smell the land.*"

"*Just follow your nose. Once you find it, you'll know.*"

"*I—*" I trailed off when I sensed something moving in the distance. One moment, it was as if the purple mist was swirling around in strange patterns, and the next I could see the gas taking on a form of its own. Faintly, beneath the patterns, I thought I could make out a shape as I might make creatures out of clouds. Then, the swirling gases started to glow, first purple, and then they brightened towards a shade of white.

I said I didn't believe in ghosts, but that's exactly what this creature looked like. Or rather like the kind of ghost that the child of my owners would dress up as every year during the autumn. He'd put a sheet over him, covering him completely except for the two slits he had cut out for eyes. This thing looked much the same, like a trailing bedsheet of light dragging along the ground.

"*Ah, you've found it,*" Salanraja said.

"*So, you can see it too, now?*"

"*Of course, I can. We're bonded, remember. What you see, I can see.*"

"*You mean you can see through my eyes?*"

"*Not quite. I only know instinctively what you're focusing on. If you listen to your senses, you'd be able to do the same thing with me.*"

The bone dragon roared out into the sky again, causing the ground to tremble. At the same time, a putrid smelling wind washed over the land. I turned up my nose, wanting to retch. Then, the Manipulator turned towards us, and I felt the sudden sensation of being watched, as if the thing was examining my very soul and trying to measure its worth in magic. The conjuration slinked forwards holding something in its hand. On closer inspection, I noticed it to be a staff just like the kind the dragon riders carried around with them. Except this one didn't have any physical shape, twisting and writhing in form alongside the rest of this wraith's body.

Meanwhile, the bone dragon wheeled around to face us in the sky. It opened its mouth and out came this strange purple flame. Strange, in the fact that it didn't glow like flame but instead looked like one column of roiling gas. Yet still it burned the reeds it touched underneath it, quickly withering them into ash.

"*Get off,*" Salanraja said.

"*What? No! It will kill me.*"

"*Do as I say. You must fight the Manipulator, while I distract the bone dragon.*"

I screeched, then I realised that I had no choice. If I didn't jump off, Salanraja would throw me off, and the latter would hurt much more. I growled as I ran down her tail and leapt off it, just as Salanraja lifted herself up into the air.

I stalked towards the Manipulator, keeping down low, trying to work out where its arms and limbs were as I moved. It saw me and pointed its staff at me, tendrils of light leaking back from its body into the head. Something then shot out of it, a bolt of purple lightning, emitting no light.

It missed me by inches and hit the ground beside me. Out of it grew these red stems and brambles shooting out in all directions. One of these brambly stems lashed out at me, and I ducked out of the way. I looked up to see that the plant had now grown a head which looked like an elephant-sized tulip with sharp white teeth that gnashed up at the sky. It lurched down with this head, in an attempt to eat me whole.

I rolled out of the way, then looked back to see it take a massive chunk of dirt from the ground. It spat it out, sending it scattering in large chunks. Then, it turned to me and let out an incredible shriek, so high-pitched it hurt my sensitive ears.

"Bengie, stay away from that thing!" Salanraja said.

"State the obvious, why don't you," I said. I dared to look up into the air to see that Salanraja was now fleeing from the bone dragon. She rolled to avoid a jet of flame coming at her tail, and it looked like it almost grazed her. I'd seen what that flame had done to the reeds in the swamp, and I was pretty sure that Salanraja wouldn't fare so well against it either.

"Hurry up and go for the Manipulator and avoid its magic!" Salanraja said. *"I can't hold on like this forever."*

Back on the ground, the Manipulator had shot out more of those bolts in random directions, and a forest of these terrible plants had risen all around me. They'd created a foliage so thick I couldn't see the Manipulator through them anymore.

That was when I heard Astravar's voice. It boomed out from somewhere behind the thorny foliage, sending a shudder down my spine.

17

A WARLOCK'S RAGE

"You fool," Astravar said, his voice filling the sky like thunder. "You're a cat, a rare breed, I admit, which is why I summoned you into this world. But now you think you can go up against an all-powerful warlock. You're just a common moggie against one of the greatest mages who has ever lived."

I tried to find a way through the thorns, keeping down low so at least I could see the manipulator. I thought I caught sight of Astravar then. His skin was blue and was cracked just like the earth beneath him. His head had replaced the head of the Manipulator, bathing within its spooky glow.

I had to get through to him, but those thorny stems still twisted all around me, lashing into the earth and ripping it apart. That terrible purple gas was now seeping out from the base of these plants. It smelled like petals rotting in a compost bin – so overwhelming and powerful it made me want to faint.

The warlock's voice boomed out again. "What should I do with you, I wonder? You might make a nice taxidermy on the wall. But no, why should I let such a supple body go to waste? You can serve as a shade, hunting the rats I summon out of the Seventh Dimension. I have a need for their husks still. Although, I think I may have found a creature to replace you."

I hissed at him and then, suddenly, a sharp pain lanced through my flank. It wasn't from those flailing thorns in front of me. I had managed to evade them thus far. Instead, I felt the end of a long skeletal claw, tearing right between Salanraja's scales. Great, I could feel her pain like it was my own. That was all I needed. I yowled out, and Salanraja let out a deep bellowing roar at the same time.

"Hurry, Bengie," Salanraja said.

"I can't get through the thorns."

Salanraja paused a moment. *"Hang on, stay low."*

A moment later, a shadow passed over me, and then an intense heat flared out from the landscape in front of me. A bright, amber fire filled the forest there, and I felt it scorching at my skin beneath my fur.

"Ow!" I said.

"Just go, you fool."

I swallowed and focused on the flames roaring in front of me. The plants writhed and thrashed within their midst. They no longer whipped out towards me, but rather at the sky in a dying effort to survive.

I had to get through them. But the flames were so hot.

But I would die if I didn't. Or worse, Astravar would have me serving under him as one of his awful minions. Maybe I'd be like that bone dragon, unable to eat because I didn't even have a stomach inside my body. I shuddered at the thought.

The flames were extending even lower now, and I knew I only had a moment before I'd be unable to pass underneath them. So, I ran forward, keeping my shoulders loose so I could squeeze through the slightest gaps. The flames dashed across my back, and I grazed something. It was a thorn belonging to one of those toxic plants. I yelped out. But I couldn't lose focus.

Astravar had now left the Manipulator, which again had the staff raised, facing the bone dragon. It was feeding some kind of energy into it, sending up a purple gaseous stream laced with tendrils of white light.

In the sky above, Salanraja had now found her way behind the bone dragon. She had a crimson gash on her flank, right where I'd felt myself get hit. Salanraja opened her mouth and let out a stream of flame, bathing the bone dragon in amber. But the flames weren't enough to kill the bone dragon. Not while the Manipulator remained.

Salanraja glanced down at me from above. *"Gracious demons, focus on the Manipulator. Distract it, and maybe I can kill this thing."*

I turned back towards the Manipulator. But it didn't seem interested in me anymore. I heard something whip from behind me, and a fiery branch was sent spinning towards me. I dived out of the way, just in the nick of time.

But with that scratch I'd taken on the leg, I felt weak and nauseous. Astravar again appeared inside the body of the manipulator, staring down from behind his cracked blue face with cruel purple eyes. "You cannot defeat me. The poison will kill you, eventually."

Yet, he didn't turn the Manipulator's staff towards me, instead focusing all its attention to casting energy towards the bone dragon.

"Take it!" Salanraja screamed out in my mind. *"While you have the opportunity."*

"Take what?"

"The crystal, you idiot! The source of its power."

I readied myself down low, and I didn't hold my position too long. The light from the Manipulator was so bright now that I couldn't see where that crystal was. But judging from the way it moved, I guessed the crystal I needed was somewhere within its chest. I crouched, then I pounced, leaping as far as I could into the Manipulator's body, which seemed to have no physical form. I'd calculated it well, and I clasped my jaws around something solid.

I landed, then continued to sprint forwards. Something tugged back at me, as if I was running against a strong gale. I could hardly breathe, but still I continued. A stream of white light surrounded me, and I found it hard to see what was beyond me.

I didn't look back.

Then, there came a whoosh of wind from above me, and some claws closed around me like a vice. They didn't belong to Salanraja. I whined out as they lifted me into the sky.

18

CAT SANDWICH

I watched the ground spin away in front of me, then I looked back at my waist to see myself gripped in a skeletal claw. It was crushing me so hard that I thought it would squeeze all the life out of me.

"*Don't let go,*" Salanraja said. "*Whatever you do, don't let go.*"

Of course, I still had the crystal within my grasp. A white stream of light trailed out from it towards that wraith-like Manipulator that slid along the ground at the same speed as us. It was as if I was pulling it along with my own mouth, and the force of it pulling back against me seemed to want to rip me in two.

"*Keep it together,*" Salanraja said. "*Hold it for long enough up there, and the bone dragon will die.*"

I didn't have the will in my mind to respond. All I could feel was the life force leaching out of me. My vision went red, and I wondered for how long I'd be able to breathe. The muscles in my mouth had by this time gone completely numb, but I didn't drop the crystal.

I felt sick, and my head was spinning, and I didn't know if it was from vertigo, or from whatever poisons that thorn had injected into me back on the ground. I mewled, and I growled, and I groaned, but still I didn't let go.

The bone dragon was now lowering itself back down to the ground. If it stayed low enough, I realised, then the manipulator might regain its energy giving the bone dragon enough strength to crush the life out of me.

Suddenly, an intense orange fire raged up from below. It burned my dangling paws, and the searing pain that rushed up made me want to open my mouth and yowl. But I had to hold on. I couldn't let go of that crystal.

"*Incoming,*" Salanraja said.

"*I wish you'd said that earlier—*"

But she wasn't talking about the fire, which the bone dragon instinctively lifted itself away from. Salanraja suddenly emerged underneath us. Then, she flapped her wings so hard that she pressed her back against the bone dragon's underbelly, sandwiching me in place. It felt like being squeezed in a vice, as she pushed upward, and the bone dragon fought with its dwindling strength to push back towards the Manipulator again. I genuinely thought I'd run out of air, and my eyes went blurry. I swear that I almost blacked out.

But Salanraja's voice brought me back to the present. "*Hold on, Bengie. Don't die on me.*"

I wasn't dead. I was hyperventilating in the bone dragon's grasp that was no longer so tight on me. I could wriggle slightly now. My skin within its claws had started to tickle. I looked up to see that each bone was fragmenting into oblivion, drifting away like embers of burnt charcoal on the wind.

"*We... Did we make it?*" I asked.

"*Conserve your strength,*" Salanraja replied. "*And just never do that again.*"

"*Never do what?*"

"*Never make me think you're going to die on me Bengie. We're bonded now, and I can't lose you. It would tear apart my soul.*"

The last vestiges of the bone dragon drifted away into the void, and the pressure lifted off of my back. I looked up into the cloudy sky, amazed to be alive. I ambled over to the edge of Salanraja's body, every muscle aching with every step I took. Down below, the forest that Astravar's Manipulator had created lay charred and dead. Those wilted stems now looked like black mummified claws sticking out of the ground.

Finally, it seemed safe to put the crystal down, and so I dropped it in between two of Salanraja's external ribs, then pawed it into a corner so it wouldn't end up falling to the ground. I was surprised how big it was. No wonder my jaw had ached carrying it.

"If you don't want me to die, don't put me in a situation where you might kill me," I replied. *"Simple solution."*

Salanraja groaned, sending a soft rumble through my legs. *"You never learn, do you? We're in this together, and it means we both need to take equal responsibilities. We'll both have to risk our lives sometimes if we're going to save this world."*

"But why should I care about your world? I wasn't born here. All I want is food, and a good rest after all that happened here."

"Because you saw what your crystal revealed, did you not? It's not just this world, but the fate of all worlds at threat. Once warlocks like Astravar control this planet, they won't stop there. Their lust for power has no bounds, and only brave souls like you and I can stop them."

I examined one of my paws and shuddered when I saw the char marks on it. *"But he's so powerful,"* I said. *"You've seen what he can do."* I tried to lick my paw so I could groom myself. But it hurt too much.

"He can be beaten," Salanraja replied. *"We have to believe that. They cannot win."*

"Whatever you say. Now, I remember you promising some food."

"Can't you ever think about anything else?"

"No..."

Salanraja laughed. But this time it sounded like a laugh of endearment rather than one of mockery.

"Fine," she said. *"Let's report our conquest to the village, and then I can hunt you something nice."*

19

MIDAR VILLAGE

Mutton was on the menu for the evening. A whole sheep, can you believe it? Though Salanraja didn't steal it or anything like that. We got it from Midar village for free.

The village elder came out to greet us as soon as we landed. It looked completely different to Dragonsbond Academy, and also completely different to the village I'd lived in in South Wales. There were no stone houses here; everything was built of wood and straw. Honestly, with these dragons flying around that could flame these buildings and roast villagers in their sleep, it surprised me they'd be so stupid as to use flammable materials for building. Still, I'd never claimed humans were smart.

The village elder was an old man, no different looking than any other old man I'd seen. He hunched over a walking stick as he hobbled over on his two feet. This time, it was a regular old walking stick, and not a magical staff like Aleam's. It didn't have any crystals on it or any of that nonsense. Honestly, it felt good to meet someone normal for a change, so I jumped off Salanraja's back, as I rubbed myself against the side of his leg, purring away.

The old man looked up at Salanraja. "Where's your rider, dragon?" he asked.

"I am the rider," I replied, and then the man jumped up in surprise and almost toppled over.

"Oh," the man said after he'd recovered himself. "You can talk... Well, with the things that come out of the Wastelands, you're not the strangest thing I've seen by far."

"And what do you mean by that?"

"Nothing." The old man shook his head and laughed nervously. "Just beings of magic and all that."

"I'm not a magical being," I said. "I'm a Bengal. A descendant of the great Asian leopard cat. You should have some respect."

The man's jaw dropped, and Salanraja let off a loud groan. *"Will you stop it with that Asian leopard cat nonsense? None of us even know what it means."*

I ignored her and instead tried to glare the old man down.

He chuckled and then reached over to scratch me under the chin. I let him, but I didn't react with any signs of endearment. I still was unsure whether or not to trust him. He smelled funny.

"So, are you the dragon rider who defeated the bone dragon? Shepherd Rala, my granddaughter, bless her, saw it die while she was out grazing her flock. Before that, it had already taken the lives of most of the flock. I'm just glad Rala got out alive." He glanced over at a small pen containing several sheep, no more.

"I am that dragon rider," I said. "You got a problem with that?"

"No, not at all," the elder replied. "So, I guess, you'll be wanting a reward. We've got a good stash of gold in our village treasury reserved for incidents like this. Or maybe, if it would please the king, he'd rather have a few hundred yarns of our Midar wool?"

I growled, softly. He just wasn't getting it. "I'm starving, and I want food." I said.

The man paused a moment, looking at me with an expression of incredulity. "You want food?"

I looked back at the pen. The sheep in there looked fat and tasty. Though they weren't lambs, I could still make do with a bit of mutton. "One of your flock should do the trick," I said.

"Bengie, are you crazy?" Salanraja said to me.

"*Shut up,*" I replied. "*I'm the one who speaks his language, so I'll make the necessary negotiations.*"

"*But they'll skin us alive at Dragonsbond Academy. We should take back some payment as a reward for the mission. It can help fund the academy and secure its future. Then they'll give you as much food as you like from the kitchens once they make you an Initiate.*"

"No," I said. "*I don't trust them, and you never seem to deliver on your promises either.*" I mewled and then rubbed my head up against the old man's leg.

Salanraja grunted, and the old man flinched, then looked at her sheepishly.

"Just ignore her," I said. "She's having a bad day. But I can tell that your village isn't the best stocked, and you need to recover from the terror. One sheep or lamb, if you have one, will do just fine."

The man tugged at the skin on the front of his neck. "Yes, well, that can be arranged, I guess." He turned back to the village and cupped his hand over his mouth. "Rala, take your fattest sheep to the slaughterhouse."

"Oh, no need," I said. "Salanraja will slaughter it herself."

"*Will I now?*"

"*You did promise to hunt something nice for me,*" I replied. "*I just thought I'd make it a little easier on you.*"

"*Gracious demons, you're an idiot...*"

The elder's granddaughter had now arrived, a tall thin woman with blonde hair, wearing a long white shepherd's frock. They were whispering between themselves. I adjusted my ears so I could hear them a little better.

"I think we can give them Colos," she said. "He'll make a fine meal, I guess." She rubbed her eyes with the back of her hand and let off a slight sniffle.

"Just point to the sheep you wish to donate, and we'll be on our way," I said.

Rala turned back to me and pointed over to the pen. "That one, eating grass by the fence. She'll be the tastiest, I think. Take her and thank you. I was so worried when I saw the bone dragon, I thought our village would be the next to fall to the Wastelands." She sniffled again.

"You're welcome," I replied, and I walked over to her and pushed my head against her shin.

But she seemed stiff and didn't really want to stroke me. So, I ran back up onto Salanraja's back. "You heard them. Take that sheep closest to the fence."

Salanraja grunted again, and then she beat her wings and flew up into the sky. The way she was behaving, I thought she was going to fly away without the sheep, but she swooped after a moment and took up the defenceless farm animal in her talons.

The sun was setting on the horizon, and it stretched across the green and yellow fields, casting its warm rays of protection as its own way of saying farewell.

20

A FEAST MOST FINE

After dropping the sheep from a great height and roasting it to mutton, Salanraja had left me to guard our meal while she went off in search of firewood. We'd camp for the night, she'd told me, and I was okay with that idea as long as we had food. Though I asked why we needed a fire when I had a fur coat to keep me warm.

But she said it was traditional on these kinds of journeys. If I was a human, I'd appreciate it. Admittedly, now darkness had fallen, the night was getting pretty cold, even for a cat.

Salanraja soon returned with a tree trunk in her claws. I looked up from my feast of mutton, which I'd already started, and licked my lips.

"Couldn't you just hold on for one minute?" she asked. *"The dragon should always get first bite of her hunt."*

"But you didn't hunt it," I said.

"I killed it. Because, I seem to recall you saying that it was far too big for you to kill yourself."

"Will you be quiet? I'm trying to enjoy my food here." I turned back to the carcass and ripped another chunk of tasty mutton off of its belly.

There came a rush of wind against my fur and I saw something massive falling fast towards me in my peripheral vision. I screeched and darted out of a way of the tree trunk, right before it thudded against the ground, sending up tufts of grass and soil.

"*What the whiskers do you think you're doing?*"

"*I said we needed firewood,*" Salanraja replied. "*And here it is.*"

"*But you could have crushed the life out of me with that thing...*"

"*Oh, I was quite careful where I dropped it, thank you very much.*" Salanraja landed on the ground next to the log and tore off some strips of bark with her teeth and claws. She moved fast, and she soon had a tall pile of loose wood on the ground between us and the mutton. She turned to this and let off a fast jet of flame at it, which ignited at once.

I watched her cautiously for a moment, but she didn't seem to be in the mood for roasting me as well as the mutton. So, I approached the carcass, tore off another strip of meat, and then I took it over in my mouth towards the fire.

Now the warmth was there, I realised how much I appreciated it. It reminded me of being back in South Wales in winter, curled up on the mistress' lap in front of the fireplace as she rocked gently back and forth on her armchair, a book in her hands. I missed that place and I couldn't help wishing that all this was a bad dream. That I'd wake up tomorrow back in my cushioned bed on the living room floor, with a breakfast of salmon trimmings waiting for me in the kitchen.

But how could I be thinking about salmon when this mutton tasted so wonderful?

"*I hope you're enjoying that,*" Salanraja said. "*Given how you damaged a poor family's livelihood to take it.*"

"It's good," I said, and I licked my lips. "*What was that you said about livelihood?*"

"*Didn't you hear them say? The bone dragon slaughtered most of their flock. They had, as I counted it, six sheep left. Before that, they probably had at least sixty.*"

"So?"

"*So, they now need to rebuild their flock and taking one of their sheep away when they have so few is going to make it much harder for them to do that. You may have ruined that family, and you don't even seem to care.*"

I dropped the mutton on the ground. Suddenly, it didn't taste so good anymore. *"Why didn't you tell me?"* I asked.

"Would it have made any difference? You would have acted the same, anyway."

"I'm not sure I would." I said. *"And I think I've had enough mutton for one day."*

"Well..." Salanraja looked into the distance. *"This is what happens when you go around acting on a whim all the time. You need to put some thought into your actions, Bengie."*

"Whatever," I replied, and I yawned. The heat from the fire was reminding me how tired I was. *"I'll know better next time."*

"That's the thing. There might not be a next time. If word gets back to the Council how you behaved there, there will go your chances of becoming an Initiate. You'll be stuck in the cattery while I'll have to ferry the king's pompous relatives across the land."

"And how long will it take for them to hear?"

"Probably when the next tax collector comes."

"Which will be?" I asked.

"At the end of the year, I should think."

"So, we've got plenty of time then, because it's not even winter yet."

"That's not the point, it's the principle of it."

"Well, my principle is I need a good night's sleep so I can present our mission's success respectably before the Council tomorrow..."

Salanraja snorted, but she said nothing more on the subject. Even though I was pretending to be nonchalant about the whole mutton incident, I did feel terrible about it. Really, though, I didn't know why. These humans had given me food when I'd needed food, and that was the way the whole cat-human relationship was meant to work.

There was a cool breeze in the air, which added a pleasant sensation to the warmth coming from the fire. Underneath this breeze, I soon drifted off to sleep.

A NIGHTMARE MOST FOUL

My body still ached from both from the burns and being crushed before, and I kept tossing and turning as I slept. But eventually, I found a comfortable spot to dream, and I saw myself in a long meadow, chasing dragonflies underneath the shade of a sad willow. The air was warm, and my master, mistress, and their son were nearby. The adults sat on a picnic blanket while the son was laughing and rolling through the grass.

Suddenly the air became chilly, and the sky took on a purple hue. A massive blue head arose from the horizon, its skin cracked like an eggshell. It looked down on me, emanating a glow like the rising sun, except this glow washed away any warmth left in the air, rendering me shivering and helpless.

I wasn't in the valley anymore. I was in a land of swamps and a purple, lifeless gas. No one was around to keep me company, other than those wisp-like creatures, the Manipulators. There must have been thousands of them scattered out across the landscape, filling it with ghostly pockets of white light. Each of them looked up as if in reverence towards Astravar's cruel face that was growing and growing in the sky. Soon, it got so large that it stretched from one end of the horizon to the other. His lips curled upward as he glared at me with those cruel grey eyes.

Then he laughed. But it wasn't a laugh of joy, it was a laugh with one sole purpose, to instil terror into the soul of anyone who heard it. To communicate that there was no greater power in this world than him. Then his gaze spun downwards and focused on me, and I had the sensation of being watched not just by him but by thousands of different creatures at once.

"You were a fool when I met you, and you remain a fool. Do you think by bonding with a dragon I won't be able to find you? Do you think you can truly escape the power of a warlock?"

My legs felt heavy and rooted to the spot, as if someone had put my feet in special manacles designed for cats. As Astravar continued to stare at me, his eyes gained a pale shade of blue, and my body felt colder and colder. I felt like I was stuck out in the snow with no shelter to hide in. I thought for a moment that I might die.

But I could not die here. I had to run. So, I mustered up strength, and pulled my legs off the ground. I didn't have my normal agility, and each step felt like I was dragging my feet through a pool of thick honey.

I trudged between the Manipulators, who each turned their heads to look down at me as I passed. I looked up at one and saw Astravar's face where the manipulator's head should be. His pale blue eyes glared down at me. His gaze seemed able to strip my life force away from me, as if he could reach inside me with his mind and yank out my soul.

I continued dragging myself along the ground, not knowing where I was going. I didn't care. I just wanted to escape. But each time I even thought I'd made some progress, I'd be right in front of a Manipulator again, staring up at it, the warlock's cruel gaze boring into me.

"Stop!" I screamed out. "Stop, stop, stop, stop, stop!"

I looked back up at the horizon. Nothing had changed. Astravar's head was still there, massive and unforgiving.

"You cannot escape me, Dragoncat," he said. "You swallowed my magic at the Versta Caverns, and now I exist burrowed inside your body where you'll never find me. Eventually I'll hunt you down, and I'll claim you back as my own."

I stopped trying to run. I had to face up to him. I had to speak my mind. "What do you want with me?" I asked. "Why did you have to bring me into this world? I had a good, comfortable home. And now you hunt me when all I want to do is live my life."

Astravar again roared out that terrible, derisive laugh. "You are such a pathetic creature," he said. "You're a scavenger who thrives on the service of others. What would your life be if I took everyone you relied on away from you? No creature that cannot survive alone deserves to live on this world, or any world for that matter."

"I'm domesticated," I said. "It's not my fault. I was born that way."

"Were you?" Astravar replied. "Because I believe you were born to be feral, and I shall make you feral again once I find you. And your dragon, she will serve me too."

I whimpered inside my throat. I hated this man. But I couldn't fight him. He was too strong.

"What do you want of me?" I said again. "Why are you here, visiting this dream?"

"I came to tell you you've failed. You disrupted an experiment when you killed my Manipulator. But if you meddle again, I will come out and destroy you with my own hands."

"An experiment?"

"A demon dragon," Astravar said. "The first one to have been brought forth from the Seventh Dimension for thousands of years. I will bring it into this world, and it will hunt down all of the dragons that protect Illumine Kingdom and convert them to my cause. You shall serve me once again, Dragoncat. Do you like the new name I've assigned to you? It's ironic, don't you think?"

An intense chill washed over me, as if an icy wind had just appeared from nowhere. It rushed past my face, and it was so strong and in my face that whichever direction I turned, I couldn't escape it. I couldn't breathe. I was going to die here. This was the end, and my life would come to nothing.

As the wind rushed past my ears, I heard him laughing in my head. He wouldn't shut up. He wouldn't go away. "Farewell, Dragoncat. Until we meet again."

I awoke into a night blanketed by cold darkness, suddenly aware of how cruel life was.

22

A TERRIBLE SICKNESS

I wasn't sure if it was because of Astravar finding me in my dream, because of the poison, or because of the crushing I'd taken when sandwiched between two dragons, but I got increasingly ill on the journey back. My fur, and probably the skin beneath, it was literally turning green, and I vomited on Salanraja's back at least three times, much to her chagrin.

Eventually, she turned her head back to me nestled in the cage. *"What is wrong with you?"* she asked.

"I don't know," I replied. I couldn't help feeling queasy.

"Probably the mutton didn't go down too well with you," she said, and barked out a laugh. *"Talk about irony."*

I wasn't in the mood for joking around. *"No, it's not that. The thorn from those toxic plants the Manipulator created. You told me not to get scratched by one, but I did. It must have gone much deeper than I thought."*

Part of me wanted to tell her about Astravar and that horrible dream. But I knew such a conversation would also lead to admitting to swallowing the golem's crystal back in the Versta Caverns. Somehow, I didn't think she'd react well to that.

It bothered me though, because what Astravar had said about the demon dragon sounded somehow significant. It really sounded like something I should tell her. But Salanraja had already said that I was in trouble with the Council of Three, and I didn't want to give her information that might make things worse.

"You should see Aleam when you land. He'll fix you up. He's good with healing and stuff," Salanraja said.

"Maybe I will," I replied. *"Or maybe I'm just going to die soon. It's been a good life, Salanraja. I had lots of salmon and roast chickens. And that mutton, even though I shouldn't have asked for it... Now, I feel complete."*

"Stop it," Salanraja replied. *"You're not going to die on me, you idiot. You've still got a lot in you yet."*

"What do you care?" I said, licking my paw.

"Because we're bonded now, and that means I care about your wellbeing, believe it or not. And I should hope you also care about mine."

But by that point, I was getting all bleary-eyed, and I soon drifted off to sleep.

I was woken up by the thud of Salanraja landing on cobblestones. I rolled down her tail before I could open my eyes, and then I yowled out when I hit the floor.

"Sorry," Salanraja said.

"Couldn't you have landed a little more softly? I was having pleasant dreams."

"No. Now just get up and see Aleam."

I picked myself up to see that we'd landed inside Salanraja's chamber. On the other side of the room, half a cow had been skinned and laid out for her. It wasn't roasted yet and, in all honesty, I didn't feel so hungry. I just felt dizzy, and a little nauseous.

"I thought you'd at least drop me off outside Aleam's door."

"What? Are you crazy? Dragons can't land inside the bailey. It's against the code."

"Why? It's not as if you'll eat anyone."

"We might," Salanraja replied. *"It hasn't been unknown."*

I groaned, and picked myself up on all fours, my legs wobbling as I stretched. I half thought they wouldn't hold me, and I'd just collapse here and die. My fur still had that green sickly hue, and it was getting even greener. What kind of disease did this, anyway? Ailments might affect a cat's eyes, nose, and ears, but I'd never known of anything to attack the fur.

But maybe Astravar was delivering on his promise early. He already had his magic inside me, and he'd injected me with his poison. Soon, if he had his way, my skin might slink off my bones and my soul might drop out of me. By tomorrow, I could be reduced to a feral skeletal cat that skulked about Dragonsbond Academy by night, murdering every living cat that I encountered.

Then, the rats here would multiply, and Astravar would work even more magic to turn them into demon rats. Dragonsbond Academy could be doomed.

It was probably the fear of what I might become that kept me padding through the bailey, following the path that Aleam had led me over just a couple of days ago. As I walked, I passed men and women, some of them in common clothes, others in uniform. All of them stared at me disdainfully as I passed. Then they backed away as if I was carrying some kind of plague.

For all I knew, I might have been.

I kept my head low as I went, half expecting an arrow to take me down from one of the walls. Then I heard some shouting from the guardhouse at the gate, and three heavyset men in shiny armour stormed over to me, shouting something. But my head was spinning so hard, I couldn't understand a word they said.

One of them lifted a sword into the air, and I was ready for it to come down on me and chop me in half. But a door opened behind me, and out of it stepped an old man in a brown robe, carrying a staff. Aleam, I recognised his voice, and he said something to the guards which calmed them down.

Aleam took me up in his arms, and he whisked me back into his study.

"What happened, Ben?" he said softly, as he stroked me under my chin. He lifted my leg and examined the cut there. "This is a Mandragora's work. You poor thing. Don't worry. The spell can be reversed if we act fast."

He dropped me onto a rug, next to the warmth of a roaring fireplace. I glanced across the long room and I caught a glimpse of Ta'ra lying on the bench. She saw me, and stood up, then jumped over the top of the sofa and hid behind it. She peeked out from behind the edge of it.

Aleam turned to look at her. "Don't worry, it's only Ben. Not a demon. He's been hurt."

"Ben?" Ta'ra said, and she walked out from behind her sofa, but still kept a safe distance. "What happened to you, you idiot?"

But I wasn't in any state to answer, because I felt a sudden wave of queasiness. The world around me was spinning, and I vomited on the floor. Shortly afterwards, I blacked out.

23

FOOD IS NOT FOR SHARING

I woke up to the smell of salmon, and for a moment I thought that I'd awoken from this terrible dream and returned home. But I hadn't, as it was Ta'ra's breath I smelled. She lay snuggled up beside me on the rug, her face right next to mine, seemingly appreciating my warmth as the fireplace had run out of fuel. I leapt right on to my feet.

"What the whiskers are you doing there, Ta'ra?" I screamed out in the cat tongue. She opened her eyes and blinked at me. I remembered then that she didn't speak cat, so I said it again in the human language.

Ta'ra yawned and then lifted herself up on all fours. She stretched, shaking as she did so, and she sat back down and gazed at me lazily.

"Oh relax," she said. "Don't you like having a pretty lady next to you?"

I arched my back. "Last time we were fighting, and now you think we're chums?"

Ta'ra yawned once again and snapped her mouth shut. She shook her head, which meant that she either had problems with her ears or she hadn't quite lost the need for that pointless humanoid gesture.

"Such a typical cat. I thought you were having interesting dreams, and I wanted to watch them for a while. I had no idea so much could go on in that little head of yours. You're very unlike the other cats here."

I snarled at her, then I said, "Weirdo."

"Whatever," Ta'ra said and stalked towards her bench.

Aleam was standing over his desk, gazing into his alembic as the solution boiled within. It had more of a green hue to it today. He was so engrossed in whatever he was doing that he didn't notice me approach until I meowed at him. He turned towards me and examined me over his glasses.

"Oh, you've awakened. Thank gracious. I thought for a while we might lose you. Salanraja looked so worried, you know. She hasn't eaten since dusk yesterday."

"Dusk," I said. "How long was I out?"

"The entire night and the morning after." Aleam said. "But after a bit of sage balm and a little white magic, I managed to get the poison out of you. Fortunately, it didn't go so deep. Just be more careful next time you ever have to fight anything like that again."

"I don't intend to," I replied. "All I want is to find a way home."

Aleam laughed. "I'm sure you will one day. Although you have to accept that it might take some time."

The alembic apparatus whistled at him and some steam rose from a pipe at the top of it. Presently, some green solution dripped out of the tap at the end into a vial. Aleam picked this up and took it over to Ta'ra who was now sitting on the sofa. "Here, drink this," he said, offering it to her.

She looked at the vial. "I'm not sure I want to. I'm starting to quite enjoy being a cat."

"What? Nonsense. You were moaning about it yesterday."

Ta'ra glanced at me, then looked away when she noticed me glaring at her. "Fine," she said. "One drop won't make much difference."

Aleam raised the vial to her mouth, and I took the opportunity to jump up on the table. The alembic was the only reflective object in sight, and I wanted to get a good look at myself. I found a spot that had plenty of liquid behind the bulb, and I examined my reflection.

Aleam had done a good job. I had my leopard-style markings back, and my skin had that beautiful amber colour to it again.

"Hey, get down from there," Aleam called out and shook his staff at me. "That's Ta'ra's cure. We can't have anything happen to it."

Ta'ra licked her lips and then examined her paw. "Whatever," she said. Something had certainly changed about her.

I jumped down from the table and I walked over to her, then I looked up at her, licking my lips. "What?" she asked.

"You, you just seem different. What's got into you?"

"I just thought that's it not that bad being a cat, that's all," Ta'ra replied. "The food's good. The humans think you're cute. As long as I can talk to them, I can be their advisor or something. I'm sure they won't assign me to catching rats."

I couldn't help but laugh, and I did so in a very human and mocking voice. "You think you'll ever learn to be a cat? You don't have it in your genes."

"Don't have what in my genes?"

"The grace. The ability to balance. You don't even know how to walk like a cat."

"Of course I do," Ta'ra said, and she jumped off the sofa and walked along the straight line between the floorboards in a particularly inelegant way. "See?"

"That's not how you do it," I replied. "Your feet don't meet."

She scowled at me. "What do you mean they don't meet? I don't want to be tripping over myself."

I groaned, then I showed her how it was done. "Your back paws should hit exactly where your front paws land, like this see?" I walked in a straight line with my head held up high. I didn't even need to focus on it – I'd been doing this since I was a kitten.

Ta'ra looked at me and blinked. "What's the point of that?"

"It makes us harder to track," I said, proudly. "It also makes us quieter. Although..." I looked down at her feet. "... you're not going to be stealthy if you don't learn to stand on your toes."

Ta'ra tucked her head inwards. "Fine, I'll practice," she said. "Maybe you can teach me to be more ladylike." She approached me and rubbed her head against my cheek. Then, she pattered over to Aleam, who was now focusing again on the alembic, and she meowed.

Aleam scratched behind her ear. Then he walked over to a high cupboard, reached inside, and tossed down some fish for Ta'ra. The aroma from it assaulted my senses. It was smoked trout!

"Hey," I called out. "What about me? I haven't eaten for ages." I didn't mention the feast of mutton that I'd gorged on before my flight back. Though, at least this fish wouldn't taste of bitter guilt.

"Very well," Aleam said. "You too." He tossed some more pink fish down on the floor, a little away from Ta'ra. As soon as he did, though, Ta'ra walked over to protect it.

I hissed at her, arching my back. "Hey that's my food," I said.

Ta'ra laughed. "No it's not. It came out of my cupboard, and so it's mine."

"What do you mean, your cupboard? Is this your floor too?" I scowled at Ta'ra.

"Will you cats stop fighting?" Aleam said. "I'm trying to concentrate."

Ta'ra looked down at the food, then she touched it with her paw. "Fine," she said. "You eat it then. But remember, I'm doing you a favour."

"And I'll teach you how to eat it properly someday," I called after her as she stalked back over to her pile of food.

Just as I'd taken a good mouthful of the fish and was starting to chew down on it, there came a banging from the doorway. The young Initiate Rine – that spotty-faced teenager – was standing there hammering the base of his staff against the floor so hard that it hurt my sensitive eardrums.

Aleam spun around from his alembic and glared at the boy. "Do you have to make such a racket?" he said. "I'm trying to work."

Rine had a grin stretched across his face that was so smarmy that I wanted to slash it off, if only I could reach that high. "I'm sorry," he said. "The Council of Three wanted me to alert you that they need your presence. Not you, Driar Aleam, the cat."

He looked down at me with that same grin and a knowing look, as if to tell me he had learned of a secret of mine. But what that secret might be, I had no idea.

"Fine," I said. "Just let me finish my food." I took another mouthful of the delicious moist fish.

"No," Initiate Rine replied. "I'm afraid they want to see you immediately, no time to eat." He walked forward and shooed me towards the door with the base of his staff.

"Hey, what do you think you're doing?"

"I said now!" Initiate Rine said.

I realised I had no choice but to follow him out of the room.

It seemed so familiar – being whisked away from my breakfast of smoked fish by an arrogant magic user. The sounds of Ta'ra's laughter followed me out the door. I didn't look over my shoulder, but I could swear she'd moved in at the first opportunity so she could go back to eating my fish.

24

FRESHCAT BEN

Salanraja was already waiting in the Council of Three's courtyard when I ducked underneath the arch to meet them. She hadn't spoken to me since I'd recovered, and I figured she was angry again about the mutton incident. Why she had to let things stew so much, I had no idea. Now, she had her nostrils flared out, was growling from the base of her chest, and I could feel her rage burning there as if it was my very own.

Really though, I didn't understand what she was so upset about. We had completed our mission, so she would look great and get the praise she wanted. Then I would become an Initiate and I'd gain the favour of the Council of Three. After that, all I needed to do was find a nice man or woman somewhere in this castle who could summon a portal for me to go home.

"Why didn't you just call me?" I said. *"Why did you have to send that annoying Initiate Rine?"*

"Because," Salanraja replied. *"All I could hear going on in your mind was food, food, food, food, food, and I knew I didn't have a chance of dragging you away from your gluttony using just my mind."*

I turned up my head. *"I would have come. The food will always be there later."*

"Will it?" Salanraja asked. *"Because I don't think you ever quite believe that."*

I whined and then turned away from the dragon. I was having a good day so far, and I didn't want her dragging me down with her negativity. This would be my moment of glory, and my opportunity to finally return home.

Driar Yila, Driar Lonamm, and Driar Brigel already had their staffs raised up to the crystal over their heads, and they were feeding their energy into it. The three Driars watched me as I moved further forward, and I looked at each Driar in an attempt to work out what they were thinking. But their faces didn't register much emotion.

"You summoned me," I said to them once I was standing right in front of their raised platform. "Here I am, and I'm sure you've heard that our mission went well. Now, if you—"

Driar Yila's sharp voice cut me off as her expression melted into a frown. "We've heard very well about your mission, and it was a complete failure as far as we're concerned."

"What?" I said, and my eyes opened wide in shock. "But we defeated the bone dragon…"

"We defeated the bone dragon, Ma'am."

I blinked at her.

"Say it," Driar Yila said. "It's about time you learned to speak respectfully."

"Fine," I said. "We defeated the bone dragon, Ma'am."

"Good. Now, from now on, remember that you shall refer to all other superiors as ma'am and sir. Is that understood?"

"As you wish," I said.

"As you wish, Ma'am."

"As you wish, Ma'am." I accompanied this with a reverent and sorrowful meow. Then, I walked up to the platform and put one foot on it, hoping that I could at least cheer them up by being cute.

"Get down off there, you filthy mongrel," Driar Yila said, and she swung her staff forwards and pointed it at me, cutting off for a moment her stream of white light that fed the crystal. I didn't want to be at the receiving end of whatever magic would be at the end of that, so I growled and then moved out of the way.

"You really know how to make a name for yourself, don't you?" Salanraja said.

I turned to her. *"I'll make it right,"* I replied. *"Where's the Manipulator's crystal?"*

"It's on my back where you left it."

"I'll get it," I said, and I sprinted around the back of her and then ran up her tail. I reached the corridor of her back, and I clasped my mouth around the crystal, then returned to the ground and dropped it right beneath the council's platform.

"You don't seem to believe we defeated the bone dragon, but I brought proof. Here is the source of the Manipulator responsible for controlling the creature. Once I stole the crystal away from the source, the bone dragon ceased to exist."

"There you go," Salanraja said. *"Take all the credit, why don't you?"*

I ignored her. I was focused on making the council happy, not her.

"So, tell us, little one," Driar Lonamm said. She leaned forward, and her broad frame cast an ominous shadow over me. "What did you do after you'd defeated this bone dragon? We know the story, but we want to hear it from the horse's mouth."

"I'm not a horse," I snapped back. "I'm a Bengal, a descendant of the great Asian leopard cat... Ma'am."

"Do you ever stop?" Salanraja chimed.

"Shut up!"

Driar Lonamm was watching me with narrowed eyes. "Fine. We heard it right from the Bengal's mouth," she said with a smirk. "Now answer my question. And before you think of lying to us, cat, know that we sent a shadow dragon rider to Midar Village to assess your eligibility as a fledgling Initiate. He followed you and he has already returned and delivered his report."

Whiskers, they knew something. I lowered my head. "I claimed my reward, Ma'am," I said. "The villagers offered me what I wanted, and so I took it."

"They offered you what you wanted?" Driar Brigel said. He no longer had that kind look on his face, but instead a rather disappointed one. "Why didn't you take what would be good for the academy and the kingdom? Tell us, do you want to serve this kingdom, or do you want to serve yourself?"

I groaned, frustrated at the idiocy of these people. "I want to go home," I screamed out. "Why is that so hard for you people to understand?"

"That's never going to happen," Driar Yila shot back. "You're a mangy, uneducated cat, and no one in this realm is going to waste powerful magic and energy on helping you cross dimensions."

Now that hurt, and not so much the part of being called mangy – even though that was an insult to my pride – but rather because I knew in my heart of hearts that Driar Yila was right. I didn't have a chance of returning home.

I lowered myself to the floor. I didn't know what to say, but I had to say something.

"Does that mean I can't become a dragon rider now?" I turned back to Salanraja, and some smoke rose out of her nostrils. She really looked like she wanted to toast me alive.

"You see, that's the problem," Driar Brigel said. "The crystal did choose you, and we can't just ignore its request. But none of us present can quite understand the reason for it."

"Because I'm a Bengal," I said and slinked out from behind my cover so I could raise my head up high. Maybe they were finally starting to understand. "But I'm not just a Bengal. From what I've learned about this place, it sounds like I'm the only Bengal in the world."

"I don't doubt you are," Driar Brigel replied, and he placed one hand on his chin. "But you are also selfish, arrogant, and unsuited for the role that has been chosen for you. Or at least, right now, it seems that way."

"So, what will you have me do? Will you send me out on another mission?" I shuddered at the thought of fighting another one of those bone dragons, or one of those golems I'd fought in the Versta Caverns. I still had that horrible taste of clay in my mouth.

"No," Driar Brigel said. "This isn't about what to do next, but your attitude about it all. Do you know what the consequences could be about the way you behaved in this village?"

"I don't," I replied.

"I believe Salanraja gave you some hints. But it's not just about the villagers. Fortunately, our Driar replaced that sheep for them."

I purred. "So, all's well that ends well."

"No," Driar Brigel snapped back. "Because unless you learn from your mistakes, you will continue to make them. Imagine what would happen if every dragon rider behaved like you did. Villagers would stop supporting the kingdom, meaning the king's realm would dry up from the inside. We'd lose funding to this academy, meaning dragon riders wouldn't get trained. That would weaken the king's forces and allow the warlocks to gain power. Negligence costs lives, you see. You need to think big in a position of responsibility, not just about yourself."

I lowered my head. When he put it that way, maybe he was right. Though I still had no idea how I could put my wishes of my tummy behind the needs of a kingdom. "I'm sorry," I said.

Driar Brigel nodded. "Admitting that is the first step, and for the first time I believe you." He looked at Driar Yila, then at Driar Lonamm, and they both gave him a nod. "So, we have decided what to do with you. You need to prove yourself to us before we even consider your schooling. We will therefore assign you a rank no one has had since we created this academy. From this day, until we feel you're ready, you will be a freshman."

"A freshman?" I said, and it wasn't the sexist nature of that rank that I objected to. "But I'm a cat."

"Fine," Driar Brigel said. "From this day on, you'll be assigned the rank of Freshcat."

"Freshcat?" Whiskers, I was making it worse. Now, I sounded like something you might order from an illegal butcher.

"Freshmoggie?" Driar Lonamm offered.

"No, no," I said. "Freshcat will do just fine."

"Very well," Driar Brigel said. "Freshcat Ben it is… Actually, I quite like the sound of that. So, from this day you can attend classes, eat in the dining hall, and you must obey the needs of any prefect or Driar on campus, as well as Initiate Rine who will serve as your temporary guardian. Is that understood?"

"Yes, sir," I said, and a cold shiver ran down my spine. Perhaps I wouldn't so much mind taking orders from the Council of Three – though they weren't particularly nice, they also didn't seem particularly needy.

But when I thought about the smarmy attitude of that Initiate Rine, someone like him would have me delivering newspapers to his feet like a dog. That was if they even had newspapers in this world, I have to admit in South Wales I always found them a little peculiar. They seemed to serve no purpose at all other than to be good for tearing up and as a cheap lining for my litter tray.

In all honesty, I couldn't understand how dogs could wrap their mouths around something that would end up in a litter tray. It was almost as bad as drinking toilet water. Dogs were disgusting creatures, really.

Anyway, I digress.

Driar Brigel stood watching me for a moment, and his look of kindness had returned to him. "Let's get this ceremony out of the way then," he said.

"Agreed," Driar Lonamm said, and Driar Yila nodded once slowly, but didn't say anything.

The three Driars raised their staffs high above their heads, and the light that streamed out of their crystals got brighter. The streams converged at a point on the front face of the crystal, and then they reflected off that point right into my chest. At first, I thought I should flee, but I was rooted to the spot, unable to move.

"Wait," Driar Yila said, and she narrowed her eyes to slits and looked right at me. "I sense something in there." The beam from her staff became red, and it suddenly felt as if something was trying to pull me back towards the crystal.

A headache pounded against my skull, and I felt like I was being searched, as if something was invading my mind and prying out all the private things in there. The pull intensified, and the surrounding air took on a strength of its own. I reached out with my claws and dug them into the stone beneath me to try to stay rooted to the spot.

Driar Lonamm's eyes shot open, and her light turned blue. "A warlock's crystal. Inside him. He's a creation of Astravar's. We've been tricked. We must kill it at once, before he does any more damage."

Driar Brigel opened his eyes a little more slowly. "Oh, I don't think he is," he said, and his light turned green. The magic lifted me into the air until I was suspended inches from the ground. The air swirled around me, becoming a strong whirlwind that beat against my sides. I felt like I was going to throw up. "See, this memory? The cat swallowed the crystal on his own will."

That was when I saw it in the crystal above my head. It was showing flashes of my memories, just as I visualised in my head. I could see myself up there, clawing clumsily against the golem as I slid around on his arm and then knocked the crystal out of his eye. Really, I'd thought I'd executed the manoeuvre more elegantly than that. It was strange seeing me from the outside.

Then I was sinking and sinking into the mud, and Salanraja lunged in to save me. But before she could reach me, the vision showed me lurching out with my head so I could cover the crystal with my mouth.

"*You fool,*" Salanraja said. "*You swallowed the crystal, and you didn't tell me about it. Gracious demons, we're finished.*"

But I didn't have the will to answer. I was just floating above the ground, pinned in place by the Council of Three's magical energy, and I couldn't wriggle, let alone think.

Suddenly the light cut off, and I fell back to the floor. I landed on my feet, fortunately; thank the whiskers for my flexible spine. But still, the landing sent a jolt of pain up through my legs and right down my back.

"What do we do now?" Driar Lonamm asked.

Driar Brigel shook his head. "We can't get the crystal out, unfortunately, as the warlock's magic has lodged it inside his body. We also can't undo the crystal's assignment and I think it would be unwise to do so."

"Still," Driar Yila said, "the cat must be kept under strict guard."

"We'll instruct Initiate Rine not to let him out of his sight," Driar Brigel said. "He's a promising young student, that one. I'm sure he'll stop any signs of the warlock trying to take control."

"Very well," Driar Lonamm said. She looked at me. "Freshcat Ben, congratulations on your new rank. However, you should have told us about this rather dire complication." She then cupped her hands over her mouth and shouted out in such a loud volume that I scurried behind Salanraja's leg.

"Initiate Rine!" she called.

There came a scuffling sound from behind me, and the spotty-faced teenager appeared at the entrance to the courtyard. "Yes, Ma'am."

"We need you to keep this cat under guard, and if you see any sign of him becoming evil, you must terminate him at once."

25

GOOD HYDRATION

After my beating from the Council, the three Great Driars dismissed me and told me to spend a little time with Initiate Rine. The spotty-faced kid didn't look too happy about it, and stared down at me with an expression of contempt. Honestly, I didn't get what his problem was. To him, I could be a useful sidekick. Having a cat around him might cause the girls around him to forget about his spots and focus on his sensitive nature. That was, if he had anything to him underneath his pompous exterior.

He walked over to the archway while the Council cut off the streams of the light from the crystal and then shuffled in their robes towards a door at the back. Brigel and Lonamm entered it, while Driar Yila turned to regard me with her harsh, scornful frown, and then she shooed me away with the back of her hand and lifted her staff slightly.

Scared of being turned into a dog or something, I decided it better to follow Initiate Rine. He was waiting for me by the archway, playing a game where he tossed a coin in the air, then landed it on the back of his hand. I followed the movements of the coin for a moment, wanting to bat it off its flight path. But it was too high up.

The young Driar looked down at me and laughed. "Whatever they say about you, you're still a cat, aren't you? I guess nothing will change that."

I narrowed my eyes. "I'm not just a cat. I'm a Bengal, a descendant of the great Asian leopard cat."

"So I've heard," Initiate Rine said. "And I'm an Alterian, descendant of the great King Zod." He flashed me an ugly, toothy grin.

I didn't like the mocking tone in his voice. "You are nothing compared to me," I told him. "You have no grace, you can't even walk in a straight line, and if I dropped you from the top of the tower you wouldn't land on your feet."

He scoffed, then looked up at the tower above us. A green dragon flew out of one of the openings high up in the tower and roared out into the sky. Driar Brigel was on the dragon, his head shining in the sun and his green-gemmed staff swinging on his back. He had managed to climb up the tower pretty quickly, and I wondered if he did so using magic.

Another dragon flew after him on its tail. This one was as yellow as lemon and had two long spikes that stuck out from both corners of its jaw. A young man sat on a saddle on its back, wearing a tabard with the symbol of a sun and moon on it over a burnished coat of silver armour. He had long black hair that whipped back behind him in the wind, and a faceted face that reminded me of one of those crystals.

"Where are they going?" I asked.

"Why's that any of your business?" Rine replied.

"Because I'm a freshcat now, one of your club."

"Exactly, which means you have to do exactly what I say, remember. To answer your question, there are rumours of something terrible out there, and Driar Brigel has probably gone to check it out."

"What exactly?" I asked. But the boy didn't reply, and so I sat down and groomed myself.

"That's right, just wait there and don't go anywhere." Initiate Rine walked over to a stone fountain and drank from the steady stream of water. I watched him for a moment, then I realised that I hadn't drunk anything for a while. I jumped up on his back and darted across it until I got to the stream. Before he could lift himself up, I perched myself on the rim of the fountain, and I caught the drops in my paw and tossed them into my mouth.

"Who said you could touch me?" Initiate Rine said, and he brushed himself off vigorously as if he thought having a strand of fur on him might kill him.

"I'm thirsty," I replied, "and you're meant to be looking after my needs."

"Wrong. I'm meant to be making sure you don't get up to no good. You've got a warlock's magic inside you and I don't want you tainting me with his evil touch."

I didn't have to listen to this nonsense. I blinked at Initiate Rine and yawned. "I'm hungry."

"How convenient," Initiate Rine replied, and looked up at the sun in the sky. "Because it's just about time for dinner. Maybe if you look at some of the younger Initiates with wide enough eyes, you'll be able to get a few scraps."

He walked off, and I followed him, the thought of food pulling at me like a leash. I'd already smelled the fish, and smoked meat, and gravy, and butter, and all the wonderful things in the kitchen here. Finally, I was going to have a chance to sample this food. I was sure at least some humans would give me some. They always did.

26

ALLERGIES

We walked through the bailey and passed Aleam's quarters. I wanted to go inside and gloat to Ta'ra that I was finally going to get a chance to dine amongst the humans. But with Initiate Rine moving with such urgency, I didn't have the chance.

He quickly turned into the corridors underneath the parapets, and he led me through them until we reached a set of double doors that led into a massive hall. A woman stood at the door, and I recognised her immediately. She was that same woman who'd attacked me with the serving spoon back in the kitchens a day or so ago.

She glared down at me over her folded arms as she tapped her huge foot on the ground.

"Matron Canda," Initiate Rine said to her with a nod.

She scowled at him. "No cats in the serving hall, Initiate Rine," she replied. "You know the rules."

"I'm sorry. But this is the Council's order. We need to keep a watch on him at all times." Rine pushed his head up to Matron Canda's thick ear and whispered in it. I turned my ears towards them. "He's got a warlock's magic inside him."

"I can hear you, you know." I told them, out loud. "I've got particularly sensitive ears."

I don't know what caused Matron Canda to jump more – what Rine had just told her or the fact that the cat by her feet could speak in the human tongue. She backed away towards one of the doors and flattened herself against it. "Go," she said. "And make sure you don't touch my plates or cause any trouble, or I'll come after you with a hot ladle of oil."

I mewled, but my action didn't seem to make her think me any less of a freak. I didn't get it, really. How could these people have such contempt towards such a cute and innocent cat? Humans are strange creatures, sometimes.

The hall had three long tables across it, each of which must have had room for feeding one hundred people. Students had gathered at the tables, sitting on the long benches as they tucked into mouth-watering plates full of turkey legs and gravy. Of course, they also had the human yucky stuff on them like potatoes, and broccoli, and carrots.

Initiate Rine moved to the table on the left, and a couple of girls his age shuffled aside to make room for him. He said something, but I didn't quite catch what it was, being so mesmerized by the plates of food. One of the girls laughed and put a hand over his shoulder, as she brushed his cheek with other.

I wasn't interested in those weird human antics. I had work to do. I just had to figure out which of these humans was most likely to give me food, and then show them the widest eyes and the saddest face. It worked every time, even with the harshest of humans, excepting Astravar.

I approached the girl who'd brushed Rine's face first, thinking if she was friendly with him, she'd also be friendly with me. I meowed up at her, and she edged away from me.

"What in the Seventh Dimension?" she said. "Rine, there's a cat in here." She sneezed, and her face went a shade of light red, which stood out quite comically against her bright blonde curls.

Rine looked down at me. "Hey stay away from Bellari," he said. "She has allergies."

The girl on the other side of Rine turned her head to me. "Aw, he's so cute," she said. "Here, kitty, kitty."

I moved over to her, and she reached down and stroked me on the back of my head with a thin finger. She was a brunette with shiny and smooth hair and a small, snub nose.

"Why, thank you," I said, purring. "Now, if you could kindly donate some turkey…"

Her jaw dropped, and her eyes went wide. "What, you talk?"

"Be careful, Ange," Rine said. "He has warlock magic inside him."

"You're kidding, never? Well, you know the rules, talking or not. We can't give you food, otherwise you'll be less effective as a ratter."

"I'm no ratter," I replied. "I'm a Bengal, descendant of the great Asian leopard cat."

"He seems proud of that," Initiate Rine said. "Such an oaf."

"Rine," the first girl, Bellari said. "Get him away, I'm not joking. Really, I could swear the warlock's magic is making it worse."

"Fine," Rine said. "Shoo, cat. Be off with you. And remember I'm keeping my eye on you."

"Oh, don't be so cruel," Ange said, and she cast Bellari a hard look. "But yeah, cat, she does have allergies, so maybe you'd be better over there." She pointed to a corner, and I looked at it, despair sinking in my chest.

"Rine's not going to tell you twice, you stupid creature," Bellari said, flailing her arms wildly in front of her. "Scat!"

I mewled, then I groaned, then I growled deeply from the stomach. Finally, I turned slowly away and slinked over to the corner they'd banished me to. I kind of wish I hadn't understood them – it would have been easier that way. I would have just sat there looking up at the food, begging until either my eyes fell out of my sockets or I got a scrap of turkey.

But I was in the wrong world. No one here respected cats. No one here gave us food or looked after us. Nobody here cared about anyone but themselves.

Time passed as I watched the students carve scraps of meat off the dwindling turkeys at the centres of the table and lift them onto their plates. They laughed, and they chattered, and occasionally one of them squealed so loudly I wished I could cover my ears. All the while, my tummy rumbled, and I felt so sad.

What had I done to deserve this torture? It was as if I was living through the worst nightmare of my life.

That was when there came a clanking of metal against the floor, and a massive young man walked into the room. I recognised him as the same man I'd seen on the citrine dragon before. He'd taken off his armour, but he still wore his metal boots and the tabard with the symbol of the sun and moon emblazoned on its front. His long black hair flowed over two heavy-looking yellow leather shoulder pads.

An older boy at the far end of the room stood up and called out, "High Prefect Lars has entered the serving hall. Please stand up and show him your respect."

27

HIGH PREFECT LARS

Q uickly the rest of the students stood up, and they all clapped together. The young man known as High Prefect Lars bowed his head, and then he put his hand out, stretching out his fingers towards the room. Everyone quietened down. This prefect, whatever a prefect was, had a tired look in his eyes and though his face had lots of hard edges to it, it was also long. He took a place at the head of the central table, next to a group of students who also had yellow shoulder pads.

Given no one even seemed to realise I was here, I thought I'd listen to his conversation. This Lars figure looked important, and I figured that if I gained some information from him, I could use it as a bargaining chip for food. A young woman and a young man sat on either side of him, but they didn't look the playful, youthful type like Rine and his two girlfriends. The young woman had short red hair, and the man had his hair cropped so short, I couldn't make out the colour.

"What news is there of the demon dragon?" the woman asked. She had her back turned to me, so I couldn't see her face.

Prefect Lars paused a moment, and he gazed towards the other end of the table, shaking his head. "It's true," he said. "Our dying Driar at Colie Town confirmed. He saw it with his own eyes."

The short-haired man lowered his head. "Will Driar Forn survive?"

"He passed just before we left," Perfect Lars replied, and he took hold of the young man's hand. "I'm sorry, Calin. I know what he meant to you."

"But, what of his dragon?" Calin replied.

"Callandras barely managed to get Driar Forn to the town before the burn on her flank took her."

Calin's face went white, and he let go of Prefect Lars' hand and turned away from the table. He wiped his face with his sleeve and then turned back to Lars, bowed, and walked hastily out of the room without even touching any turkey.

The woman leaned forwards towards Lars and put a hand on his knee. "I'm sorry, Lars," she said. "It must have been hard for you."

"We just need to stop Astravar," he said. "But no one knows where he might be right now. He flew off on a bone dragon right after he'd almost killed Driar Forn."

"But where's he getting his power from? He can't use the life force of anything in this realm."

"Demon rats," Prefect Lars replied.

"What?" the woman replied.

I backed away from their table and hid under the adjacent table. It was me who'd summoned the demon rats, and so I felt partly as if I was to blame.

"Driar Brigel told me all about it on the way back. Astravar's been experimenting in using creatures from other dimensions. He summoned a cat from the Third Dimension, which I believe is some-where in this castle. Then he used that cat to kill the rats he summoned from the Seventh Dimension. They're tough rats, as you probably know, but I hear it's also a tough cat. After Astravar gained a large enough stack, he could use them for an even greater summoning."

"It's terrible," the woman said, shaking her head.

"That's not all," Lars said. "Driar Forn discovered on his mission that Astravar has enough summoning power to call up a demon dragon."

"A demon dragon? But you can't kill them, can you? It will destroy us all..." the woman lifted her hand to her face.

"I fear a war is coming, Asinda," Prefect Lars replied, then he lowered his voice to almost a whisper. "And, yes you're right... It's not one that we can win. Not if the warlocks have a dragon like that at their disposal."

Whiskers, I'd heard enough. All those demon rats I'd killed, and at the time I thought I'd been doing someone good service. Not only did they taste disgusting, but Astravar was planning to use it to conjure the demon dragon that would destroy this world. Then, if they were right, the creature would also destroy my world.

But not just that, it would destroy the entire universe's supply of food, and here I was, the creature who assisted Astravar in this deed. Really, I wasn't surprised that these humans hated me so much.

I pulled myself out from underneath the table, brushing against a female student's bare calf who shrieked as if she'd just seen a hippopotamus. The young lady talking to Lars, Asinda, turned sharply around and glared at me through two intense cornflower blue eyes. I regarded her a moment, and then I remembered that I was the enemy here.

So, I dashed to the other end of the room, and I retreated back to the corner that I'd been banished to. I watched with sadness as the students devoured the rest of the turkey. I wanted to eat some, but at the same time I knew I didn't deserve it.

Eventually, the students finished up, and they filed out of the room, leaving their plates bare on the table. An army of serving maids came in and quickly whisked the plates away. Soon, it was just me, Initiate Rine, and his girlfriend Bellari left in the room.

He kissed her on the mouth, and then he stood up and moved towards me.

"Not him again," Bellari said.

"I've been assigned to look after him," Rine replied. "What can I do?"

"Please, just don't get any of him on you. You know it's not good for me. I'll see you tomorrow, okay?" She kissed Rine on the lips again, and then rushed out the door.

Initiate Rine approached me, the sound of his footsteps echoing off the walls. "What are you looking so sad about?" he asked.

"Don't you humans think cats always look sad?" I hadn't known facts like this before I came to this world. But along with the language, the crystals had gifted me with a little knowledge of how humans think.

"You do," Rine replied, "and I've never known why. So, did you manage to get any food out of anyone?"

"I didn't feel like it," I replied. "Besides, your girlfriend said no one was allowed to feed me. Aren't I meant to be chasing rats or something?"

"Yes, about that. Don't let Bellari get to you. She's harsh sometimes, but once you get to know her she's sweet, and she's so beautiful, don't you think?"

I blinked at Rine. "Are you really doing this?" I asked.

"What?"

"Apologising to me."

Initiate Rine glanced over his shoulder towards the door. "I just thought you'd appreciate it."

I meowed, and then I brushed my cheek against his trouser leg. It finally felt good to have some sympathy around here, and I thought that maybe if I could appeal to Rine's soft side, maybe things would be a little easier. Plus, given how horrible his girlfriend had been to me, it made sense to get as much of myself on his clothes as possible. That would teach her a lesson.

He chuckled and then reached down and tickled me at the back of my neck. I rolled over on my back, and he rubbed my tummy. Maybe this boy wasn't so bad after all.

"You know," I said. "Maybe that Bellari girl isn't as great a potential mate as you think."

"I don't think any of the other boys think that." Rine winked at me.

"But what about the other one, Ange? I think she's much more suitable. Her genes are better."

Rine raised an eyebrow at me. "What are you talking about?"

"Think about it. Do you really want your children to grow up with cat allergies? You never know, first it might be cats, then dragons."

"Don't be stupid. No one's allergic to dragons."

"That's what you think."

He laughed again, then he lifted himself up and reached into a pouch on his hip. "You know, you're quite entertaining. Say, I don't usually do this. But seeing you over there, I couldn't help but feel sorry for you."

Out of the pouch, he produced a massive scrap of turkey, with the skin on it and all. I looked up at it and started meowing. He dangled it above my head, and I tried to bat it out of his hands with my paw. But he raised it out of reach whenever he saw me move.

Whiskers, it was so annoying when humans did that.

"Please," I said. "I'm starving."

"Okay," Rine replied. "You said the magic word." He dropped the turkey on the floor. I pounced upon it and tore it up into pieces with my tongue and my teeth. It tasted so good – the best meat I'd had for days. I don't mean to say anything bad about Salanraja or anything, but she wasn't much of a chef.

"Hey," I heard someone call out from the doorway, and heavy footsteps stomped towards me. It was that horrible woman, Matron Canda. "I thought I told you not to feed the cats."

Initiate Rine put his hands on hips and turned to her. "No," he replied. "I believe what you said was not to let him eat off any of your plates. But look at this… He's eating off the floor."

"Fine," Matron Canda replied. "Just hurry up out of here. I want to lock up and get a nap."

It didn't matter, because I'd pretty much finished eating. Initiate Rine shrugged, and I followed him out of the door.

28

DORMITORY

I t's strange, I'd been so hungry back at the kitchen that I'd completely forgotten about that conversation Prefect Lars had had with his friends. But as I strolled with Rine through the corridors, at first looking up in pride as the boys and girls pointed at me and giggled, I started to feel guiltier and guiltier and I sank my head in shame. Like the mutton had previously, the turkey now left a sour tang on my tongue. Food just didn't taste the same when you didn't feel you deserved it.

Rine led me through the corridor and down a stone spiral staircase with steep steps into a dark corridor lit by lights that reeked of oil. By the time we reached the boy's chambers, I found it hard to drag one foot in front of the other, I was so demotivated. My head, and my legs, and my stomach all felt like lead, and I wanted to curl up in a corner and have a good sulky sleep.

Initiate Rine took a key from his pouch. It was the size of his hand – much bigger than anything I'd seen my master and mistress use in South Wales. He put the key into a wide keyhole, and the door creaked open to reveal his dormitory room.

We stepped inside, and I started to explore Rine's territory, sniffing out every nook and cranny, as you should when you first discover a new place.

One thing I could say about my old place in South Wales was it had so much room for running around in. Even the child's bedroom had a nice armchair for scratching and a tall double bed I could hide under. But Rine didn't have any of that.

His room was boxy and as soon as I felt the air flowing out from the darkness against my whiskers, I could taste the mould in there. He had a single bed, neatly lain with a woollen grey blanket. There wasn't much else in the room except a bookcase, a small round table with a candle on it, a heavy wardrobe, and a rack for placing his staff. Rine took a match from a box on the table and lit the candle, suffusing the room in a warm flickering light.

"You don't have a bathroom?" I asked.

Initiate Rine cocked his head. "The bathhouse is upstairs. But I thought cats hated water."

"Not a bathhouse. A bathroom. You know, a place where you can have a shower but also go to relieve yourself."

"The latrine's down the corridor. But it's for humans only." Rine shut and locked the door.

"But where am I meant to go if I need to relieve myself? You don't even have a litter tray."

"Don't tell me you need to go already? I would have thought you'd do so outside."

I groaned, and then I found a spot under the table that looked suitable. I rubbed against the wall there to mark it with my scent, so I'd remember it later.

Meanwhile, Initiate Rine had opened the wardrobe and was rummaging around inside it. He threw a few clothes out onto the bed, and then he produced a second blanket, looking just as dull as the first. "Here. You can use this as a bed. I think it will be comfortable enough."

I purred and brushed against his leg, and he reached down and stroked me. He then placed the blanket underneath the table. "Not there, for whisker's sake," I said.

"Why not?" I wanted to tell him that litter spots were meant for cockroaches, not cats. But I thought it wiser to keep my trap shut.

"Nothing," I replied. "It's just I prefer this spot by the wardrobe. It's cooler, and I have less chance of burning to death if someone knocks that candle over."

"And why might someone do that?"

"I don't know… They might get a little bored." I licked my paw.

"You're a funny creature," Rine said, and he kicked out the blanket with his foot and then shuffled it over to the place by the wardrobe. I yawned as I watched him iron out the creases with his foot. I was starting to see a new side to Initiate Rine, and I liked it. When he wasn't showing off around the girls, he seemed to know how to care for cats. If I could only find a human like him outside of this castle, maybe I could have a good life in this world.

I found I was so tired that I just stepped over to the blanket, padded the creases back into it again, and then I lay down for an afternoon nap. I dreamed sweet dreams of running through a field of long grass towards Salanraja and then jumping on her back. She took off into flight and we sailed through the sky.

Part of me expected to see Astravar in every cloud we passed. I expected to hear his voice in my head and listen to him gloat about how he was summoning a demon dragon using the otherworldly rats that I killed for him. It was strange. Part of me felt that Astravar belonged in that dream. But he wasn't there. It was almost as if someone was protecting me from him entering my mind.

Still, my guilt caused me to sleep fitfully. I woke to see that the candle had been extinguished. But I could still see in here, due to a little light spilling in beneath the bottom of the door. Initiate Rine lay in his bed, fast asleep. But now I couldn't sleep, and so I looked around for something I could use to sharpen my claws.

I tried scratching at the blanket, but I didn't like the way it felt. I tried the wardrobe, but the wood there was too solid for me to gain any traction. Same with the table, and the chair, and the rack for the staff I could only just reach the bottom of. It felt unnatural almost, as if everything in the room had been augmented with magic to make it undamageable.

"*You are so loud at night,*" Salanraja said. "*Why can't you just stay asleep?*"

"*I can't help it, I'm nocturnal.*"

"*Then learn not to be. It's not as if there's anything to hunt in Initiate Rine's room.*"

I scented a cat outside the door, and I heard it stalk by. In a way, I wished I was out on duty hunting rats with it. Maybe I belonged out there. After all, that's what the descendant of the great Asian leopard cat should be doing at night, hunting. But instead, I was here unable to do a thing – the cat that had contributed to the inevitable annihilation of the universe.

"*You're so negative lately,*" Salanraja said. "*Can you not think about something a little more motivational?*"

"*What? You can hear my thoughts?*"

"*I can hear the ones that you shout loud enough. They're full of all kinds of little secrets. Which is one of the reasons I'm so frustrated with you. Humans trust dragons to share their worries and help them through problems. But you seem to want to keep everything bottled inside.*"

"*So, you know about the demon rats?*" I asked.

"*I do... You should have told me. The more information I have, the more I can communicate to the Dragon Council about what to do next. But you kept that part about swallowing that crystal a little quiet inside your head. You didn't even seem to want to think about it.*"

I curled up into a ball. "*So, what am I going to do about it?*" I asked. "*Astravar can just take control at any time, can't he? What if I lose control of myself completely? What if he turns me into a demon cat?*"

"*Don't be stupid, he can't turn you into a demon. Demons were born in the Seventh Dimension and they must be summoned from there.*" Salanraja sounded frustrated. "*I don't know what it means. You're dangerous, yes, we know that. But you're going to have to learn to deal with it by yourself. Now let me get some sleep.*"

I growled, and then I went back to whispering in my thoughts.

That seemed to be the way to stop her prying, and also for me to let her get the sleep she 'needed'.

Really though, I didn't want her to cotton on to what I was planning. Because I knew I couldn't stay in Dragonsbond Academy any longer. I didn't belong here. I belonged in the wild, like my great Asian leopard cat ancestors. Either I would learn to survive there or die.

I walked over to the door and tried scratching at it. If Rine hadn't locked it properly, maybe I could paw it open and sneak out. But I wasn't so lucky. I had to revert to Plan B instead.

Initiate Rine was now facing towards me on his bed. His mouth was wide open, and he was snoring from the bottom of his throat. I meowed so loudly you could probably call it a yowl. Then I jumped on to a spot on the mattress right by his stomach, and I crawled on top of Rine and put my mouth to his ear.

"Initiate Rine," I said and meowed a couple more times. "Wake up, it's important."

He pushed me away. "More sleep," he said. "No, not there, Ange… Please, Ange…"

"Now Rine," I said, and I walked back up to his ear and then licked it. When a cat wanted to wake you up, he meant it.

Rine opened his eyes, and I dropped down in front of him and looked right into them. "What in the Seventh Dimension?" he asked.

"I need to go to the toilet," I replied.

"Oh, just go under the table or something. The cleaner will clean it up in the morning."

"Please," I said. "I can't hold it in any longer."

Rine raised his voice. "I said just go underneath the table."

"But I can't do it there. I must do it on something soft. This bed looks perfect…"

"No!" Rine replied, and he slung his legs around and put his feet on the floor. "Oh, you are such a pain in the bum."

I jumped off the bed and stood by the door. "Oh, thank you, Rine," I said. "But if you would hurry up, I'd be so eternally grateful. Really, I'm not sure how long I can hold on. It's a matter of life and death."

"Give me a moment." Rine rubbed his eyes with the back of his hand and yawned. He put his slippers on and walked over to lift the key off a hook on the side of the wardrobe. He took hold of his staff at the same time.

"Stay with me," he said as he unlocked the door. "I wish I had a leash or something."

I followed him obediently into the light of the corridor, looking up at the cold blue crystal on his staff as we walked. I didn't want to find out what he could do with that, and so I didn't plan on trying to run away from him. Or at least not while he was looking.

He led me out into the bailey, and then he stopped and leaned against the wall. The air had a breeze on it which was frigid enough to create frost. I looked up at Rine, and I licked my lips.

"Come on," Rine said, tapping the butt of his staff against the cobblestones. "Or are you telling me you don't want to go after all?"

I turned towards the thin crescent of the moon. The silhouette of a cat stalked in front of it over one of the walls. A rat scurried down the stone, but it wasn't fast enough for the cat which caught it within its claws and then squealed in delight.

"Ben," Rine said. "You're really making me want to cook you alive."

I turned back to him. "I can't go while you watch. I need at least some privacy."

"What?" Rine said. "You're a cat for demons' sake."

"I'm not just a cat," I replied, and I almost used the great Asian leopard cat line, but I realised just in the nick of time it probably wouldn't work.

"I'm a talking cat," I continued. "Which means you should treat me with more respect than a normal cat. I mean it. Turn away. Otherwise, we'll be here all night."

"Fine," Rine replied, and he turned his eyes upwards and whistled.

"No peeking, now," I said.

"I'm not looking."

"Not even from the corner of your eye?"

"Not one bit," Rine said.

I didn't believe him. But this was the best chance I was going to have. So, I crept slowly towards the wall, looking out for a shadow I could use to my advantage. But Rine had been smart and taken me to a place fully covered by the moonlight, and there wasn't a cloud to be seen in the sky.

I started scratching at the ground, behaving very catlike as if I was preparing the terrain to receive its offering. All the while, I kept one eye on Rine as I scanned the wall for a way up with the other. Clearly it wouldn't be easy for a human to climb. But I wasn't a human.

"Rine, are you sure you're not looking?"

"I'm not," he replied. He had his staff clutched in both hands now, and I could see his arm muscles were tense underneath the folds of his clothing. Whiskers, he was expecting me to try something. Fortunately, I remembered a little something he said in his sleep.

"I thought I said I didn't want anyone looking," I said.

"I'm not…"

"Not you. Ange."

"What, where?" Rine sharply turned his head away from me.

"Over there by the fountain," I replied. "Fooled you!"

I scarpered up onto the wall and caught the stone rim at the top, which I grappled with all the strength I had in my paws.

29

TO SWIM OR NOT TO SWIM?

The wall wasn't as easy to climb as I thought it would be. I must have lost a lot of my strength, because I'd had plenty of practice climbing up the loose stones of the castle on the hill back in South Wales. Us cats used to gather there and have all kinds of competitions. I won most of them until the Savannah cats arrived in the neighbourhood.

The moonlight and the long shadows had made the stones on this wall in Dragonsbond Academy seem to stick out much further than they actually did. So, when I got to the top, my shoulder muscles were screaming out at me in pain. But I made it and pulled myself over.

But by the time I did, Rine had worked out that I'd created a decoy and there was no Ange waiting nearby ready to steal his affection.

"Hey!" he yelled, and he raised his staff. Something cold and blue shot out from his crystal. I ducked behind a parapet so it didn't hit me, and shards of ice erupted from the stone.

I continued to run along the wall, hoping that I could just jump down the other side. But the moat was down there, and I really didn't want to have to leap into water, particularly given how cold it was. From this height, I wouldn't have a chance of catching myself on the steep bank, even with the balance of a cat.

So, I darted my way along the parapets. A guard blocked my path. He wore shiny armour and a cone shaped helmet with a ridiculous looking nose-guard protruding from it. Really, those helmets made the guards look like elephants with half their trunk missing. But I didn't have time to stop and mock. I weaved my way between the guard's feet and carried out along the *chemin de ronde*. It wouldn't be long until he realised the commotion that Rine was causing below the wall was about me.

I found a staircase at the end of the *chemin de ronde* and I sprinted down it. I reached the bottom. The door was open in the guardhouse, but I wasn't interested in that. Instead, I sprinted towards the portcullis, hoping to squeeze underneath it.

But when I narrowed my shoulders and pushed as hard as I could, I couldn't make it past my belly. Whiskers, I had far too much mutton and turkey inside me. It was as if Salanraja and Rine had planned this to trap me in here. If they fattened me up, I'd have no chance of escape.

I growled, and I groaned and pushed even harder. But my efforts achieved nothing.

"Stop right there, Ben," Initiate Rine said from behind me. "Take one step further and I'll freeze your bum."

I froze stock still, and I listened to the clanking metal boots and armour coming from the guardhouse. "Captain Onus here," a man with a gruff voice said. "Am I to understand, young Initiate, that you've woken up the entire guard because of a cat."

"That isn't any old cat," Rine replied. "He's a descendant of the great Asian leopard cat."

"What?" Onus said.

"He's special. And the Council of Three have ordered that he must not leave this castle. This is a matter of great importance, Captain." The whole *swallowed a warlock's crystal* thing must have been top-secret, as he didn't mention it. This was probably for the best, really.

"It's a cat," another guard said, this time female.

"Just seize him," Rine said. "I know I'm a kid, but these aren't my orders."

"Fine," Onus said. "I'll do it myself. I'm good with cats."

Rough hands grasped me from behind, and they tugged me out of the portcullis, with such force I thought he would rip my shoulders off. One thing was clear, this man wasn't as good with cats as he claimed.

His hands moved up to my waist, and he lifted me up to examine me from below. The guard captain had a pockmarked face, with lips far too big for it and a nose that looked like someone had twisted it at a right angle and then put it back again. I kept my cool and didn't wriggle and scratch, despite how much his tight grip was hurting me. I needed time to work out what to do next.

"I'd be careful," Rine said with an undertone of cheekiness. "I only brought him out here because he needed to go, and he hasn't done so yet."

The captain pursed his massive lips at me. "Here, kitty, kitty. I guess the moat makes a good toilet, does it?"

Rine sighed from behind me. "I doubt it. Tell him, Ben. In fact, tell us all why exactly you wanted to escape?"

But I kept quiet. I wanted to save the element of surprise for the most apt moment. The guard captain moved me to the side a little so he could look at Rine. "Initiate, did the chef give you the wrong kind of mushrooms today?"

"This cat talks," Rine replied. "That's one reason he's so important to us. Ben, say something."

"There have been rumours of talking cats in this castle," the female guard pointed out.

"And I've already told you that this rumour is nonsense," Onus replied. "Besides, how could something so cute cause so much trouble?"

The captain moved me a little closer and tickled me under my chin. Unfortunately, even with my special language abilities, I didn't seem able to fake a purr. But it seemed Captain Onus didn't need one to assume that I liked him. "He might be crazy, but you don't seem crazy, do you?"

"Okay, that's enough," Initiate Rine said, and I turned to see him extend his arms. "Here, hand him over. Ben, I won't let you out of my sight again."

"What do you think, little kitty? Do you think this man is safe?"

But I could see that Rine had the authority here. So, I didn't have much time.

I hissed at the guard. "I think both your name and your face are only one vowel away from looking like a bottom," I said, and I swiped at him hard with my claw. I hit him on the cheek before he shouted out in shock and dropped me on the cold stone ground. Of course, I landed on my feet.

"You buffoon," Initiate Rine said. "Stop him!"

But the guards weren't fast enough to react as I darted between their legs and scrambled back up the staircase to the *chemin de ronde*. I passed the first corner tower, and then I took a sharp right and balanced myself on the crenel. Heavy footsteps resounded from behind me, clanging urgently against stone.

I looked down at the water, and I shivered as I imagined the cold of it. But I really didn't have much choice. Something icy and sharp whizzed by me, just as I leapt off the wall. I didn't land in the water. I landed on the steep bank, hurting my knee as I rolled down.

The water was freezing and shocking, and it tasted like mud. But still I swam towards the opposite bank, rage and adrenaline pushing me forwards. I didn't look back as I scrambled up the side and then I ran into the darkness, the moon now hidden behind a cloud.

Some arrows followed in my wake alongside some sharp looking icicles. But through speed, and darkness, and the fact I wasn't exactly the largest of targets, I escaped out into the wild world.

30

ROAMING THE WILDS

I don't know for how long I continued to run. It must have been for hours. As I did, the clouds continued to build in the sky, and I could feel the humidity on my whiskers threatening rain.

I had a stitch in my side because of all the food I'd eaten lately. But I needed to get far away from Dragonsbond Academy. For all I knew, there could have been dragons up there, hunting me from the sky. I had no doubt that with their massive eyes, they could see well in the dark. But I couldn't see anything hovering above.

Ages later, I found a forest. I couldn't see the trees, but I could sense them. The way the wind rolled through forests felt different against my whiskers than it did over the plains. I continued onwards until I knew I was underneath the tree cover. It was warmer in the forest, though I listened out for wolves or anything that might want to take advantage of a smaller cat. Here, I felt naked and vulnerable. There was bound to be something bigger than me here, ready to tear me apart.

Salanraja had mentioned all kinds of dangerous beasts – chimeras, Sabre-Tooth tigers. All the while she would be back at Dragonsbond Academy, dreaming away, not realising what danger I might be in. Whiskers, knowing my luck, I might come face to face with a hippopotamus. It would tear me apart with its razor-sharp buck teeth before I even saw it.

I decided it better to put all my worries behind me, because I was tired, and I really needed rest. I searched around for soft underbrush, which I then patted down with my paws. Once I lay down, I fell asleep almost instantaneously.

Astravar watched me in my dreams.

In them, I was once again running through the darkness. I couldn't quite see it, but I could sense it in the sky, a massive grey eye blinking the rain and the wind away. It rolled around and watched me wherever I stepped. No matter where I went – behind trees, into caves, through swamps, it was always there. I couldn't escape him.

There was no sunrise to wake me, only a sombre wall of grey cloud and a chilling drizzle in the air. It seemed to seep into my bones, and so it was hard to lift myself onto all fours and get moving again. But after all the exercise, I was also famished.

I started by eating woodlice. It was absolutely disgusting, and I knew I wouldn't go far on such tiny bugs. But they were easy to find under logs and stones, and they gave me enough energy to continue onwards.

Soon, I was ready to stalk the land for larger prey. But no rabbits or birds or even mice wanted to come out and play in this disgusting weather. I couldn't see anything. I couldn't hear anything. Whiskers, I couldn't even smell anything. So, I continued to walk through long, cold, and wet grass, looking out for even the slightest movement.

"It doesn't matter where you go, Dragoncat," his voice said in my head. *"You will always need help. You will never learn how to survive alone."*

I tried to ignore the voice, but it droned on and on through my head, telling me how useless and pathetic I was. It was as if, through some kind of magic, the warlock was causing every single living creature to hide away. Maybe he was even causing this terrible weather. But was he that powerful?

After I'd hunted for what must have been a couple of hours, without success, all I wanted to do was collapse. I lay down in the grass, meowing to no one in particular. I was just about ready to curl up and die.

That was when Astravar decided to throw me a bone. *"What would you like to eat little one,"* he asked. *"Perhaps some rabbit?"*

My eyes were so bleary that I wasn't sure if I saw it for real or imagined it. But, all of a sudden, a purple tiny creature that looked something like a sparrow except with butterfly wings and a human-looking face appeared on my nose. She laughed so loudly that her voice seemed to ring in my ears, and she fluttered away, a trail of purple glowing dust streaking behind her.

Then, she sprung up into the air like a rocket, and came back down again. She dived right into a hole in the ground. A rabbit hole…

The ground shook, and a white rabbit came out and gazed blankly ahead. I didn't even care where it had come from. I crouched down and readied myself. It twitched its ears and sniffed at the air, but it didn't seem to notice me stalking through the long grass.

I curled up my hind legs, then I pounced forwards. It tried to run away at the last minute. But it was too late. I kept it pinned with my claws, and I don't know what happened next. I remember wild thoughts going around my mind. I saw red, I tasted iron on my tongue, and my nostrils filled with the scent of something sweet and, in retrospect, sickly. I tore into the flesh with claws and teeth, and the grass bowed around me as a strong and icy wind rolled through the vale. Clouds boiled in the sky, thunder booming out of them. Soon, the fields became sodden with virgin rain.

I woke up from my trance feeling strong, satisfied, a powerful beast of the wild. My ancestors, at that moment, must have stirred in their graves.

The rain had stopped by that point. Beneath me was a carcass, almost completely stripped of flesh. Flies buzzed around it and vultures wheeled overhead. But they wouldn't dare come down until this beast of the wild, the great Bengal of South Wales, had abandoned his feast.

I gave them permission by turning away from the carcass and walking through the wild grass. *"That's it, Dragoncat,"* Astravar said in my head, and I wanted him to be there. *This is truly what it means to be wild and free. Now come, and we shall explore the world together.*

I didn't feel afraid. Nor did I feel ashamed to have abandoned my friends and my dragon back at the academy. After all, humans were worthless creatures who tried to exploit cats like me for their own benefit. But what they never realised was that it was actually the cats that exploited them.

I felt truly complete, as if I was pursuing my destiny as a hidden force inside me pulled me onwards. It was as if there was something solid in my head, right in front of my nose that was acting as a compass. It told me exactly where I needed to go, and I only needed to follow it.

I crossed over into a swampland where a purple gas rose from the reedy plants and the water. There was something about this that was absolutely intoxicating. This was where a wild Bengal truly belonged.

But all this while, the world was gaining clarity, as if I was just emerging from an incredibly vivid dream.

31

SCORPIONS AND SPIDERS

The intoxication wore off eventually as I delved deeper into the Wastelands, and a sinking realisation came over me that I shouldn't have gone so far. I wanted to turn around and go back. But that was the thing, I'd lost that directional compass at the front of my nose and I really didn't remember the way I'd come.

What a fool I'd been. How had I allowed myself to get tricked like this? But Astravar had used my mind to get me here. He was leading me into a trap which I was sure I'd spring any moment now, and without knowing exactly where the tripwire might be, I had no chance of escape. I should have listened to Salanraja. I should have listened to the Council. But instead, I just had to go around doing things my own way.

Astravar had stopped talking in my head by that point, and so I was completely alone as I continually cursed myself for my stupidity. The purple gas didn't just rise out of the ground, but it seemed to follow me. It twisted into shapes as I went, almost as if it had magic inside it. Every so often, I'd get the creepy sensation of something watching me, and then I swear I would turn around and see something humanoid dissolve into the mist.

After a moment, I could hear the sounds of skittering feet and then a chittering that sounded like magpies cackling at ten times their normal speed and volume. I spun around in circles until I was dizzy, trying to identify the source of the sound. But the purple mist was getting denser all around me, and I could see nothing.

More chittering came out of the murk, as if the sound had formed a cloud itself. When I thought I could hear it coming from one direction, another sound would emerge behind me. It's as if there were evil creatures in the mist that wanted to toy with me. They wanted to see how much they could agitate poor Ben.

That was when I saw the first of them. A bulky arthropod armoured with interlaced plates of slimy chitin, and a tail that towered up as high as a telephone pole. A massive purple bulb teetered at the top of the tail, with a long black sting shooting out of the front of it. The creature had two fat pincers on either side of it, with sharp blades on them, making them look like incredibly sharp scissors. Although I couldn't see any eyeballs within the creature's narrow jet-black eyes to show where it was looking, I knew it had its gaze affixed on me.

It sped forwards on its long spiny legs. I didn't even think about it. I darted away before it could plunge its sting into me. It hissed, and I ran as far towards the horizon as I could, not caring anymore where I was going.

But another of these creatures blocked my path. I turned to be again blocked by another, then another. They seemed to be crowding around from all directions, the ethereal purple mist swirling around them as if it belonged to them.

"You know," Astravar said in my head. "These were such fun to conjure. In my land, you call them serkets. But oh, how I've studied your world from afar. Once upon a time there, I believe a desert princess summoned one, and the people worshipped it as a god. Alas now, all you have on your planet is measly little scorpions. You are used to a world that's so tame."

The serkets continued to close in around me, their massive stings wavering in the air. I tried to look for a gap through them. I might have been able to make it past one, but many more were closing in from behind the front row. The monsters continued to shuffle around until they had me surrounded in a horseshoe formation, opening at a massive crag that rose high into the sky. There was nowhere to go but a cave mouth, shrouded in complete darkness.

I backed into this darkness, shivering at a sudden wave of cold washing over me. The serkets continued to chitter and snap their pincers, ever more unnerving as I couldn't see them now.

It was so dark in the cave that I couldn't navigate by sight. But I had my sense of smell, and I had my whiskers to detect the variations in the air currents. I didn't want to run as the ground was slippery. But I kept my ears attuned to the serkets behind me, making sure they kept their distance.

The cold air flowed through the cave, and I knew there must be an exit somewhere further in. But not a sliver of light came from within. I heard bats squealing away, and I wondered if some of them were those horrible vampire bats that the Savannah cats had told me about. Those things, they said, could tear off your flesh in your sleep. They weren't as scary as the hippopotamus but terrifying all the same.

Suddenly, something sticky brushed against my nose. Yeuch, a cobweb. There would have to be spiders in here. I'd been bitten by a wolf spider once, and it hurt so much I thought I was going to die.

I turned around, considering backing back into the serkets. But I could hear them inside the cave now, and I didn't fancy my chances of ducking away from their stings in the dark.

I swiped the cobwebs away with my paw and continued onwards. But the stickiness got worse and worse, and before I knew it, I couldn't move forwards. I struggled in the dark, trying to claw away the cobwebs, but I ended up getting further entangled. Soon, I found myself half suspended off the ground, and I couldn't budge a muscle.

I mewled, and I groaned, as I waited for the horrible sting of a serket to pierce my flesh. Those things looked like they'd have so much venom inside them, they'd kill me in an instant. I just hoped it would be painless. There was no point struggling anymore. This was finally my time to die.

Then, a light came on, green and witchlike. It wasn't coming from a crystal, or a torch, or an oil lamp, or anything like that. It belonged to the body of something massive and swollen. The light emanated out of a creature's abdomen, which was even bigger than each of the serkets that had now crowded around as if part of a religious congregation. This glowing belly belonged to a spider with eight hairy legs as big as tree trunks, eight eyes that looked like polished stones, and two raised fangs which dripped with a glowing green substance.

This wasn't a wolf spider. This was the biggest spider I'd ever seen. It smelled of all the things that nature shouldn't smell of – like a dustbin full of food that had been left alone in the heat for months.

"You really were a disappointment to me, Dragoncat," Astravar said in my mind. *"I thought you might even put up a small fight. But don't worry, my pets will strip the flesh off you and then we'll reanimate you in a new form. You shall soon become the creature you were meant to be. Wild, and undead, and so powerful that you won't even need a soul."*

I thought the spider was going to tear me apart with one of those massive fangs. But instead, it crawled a little along the web, and then it spat some venom in my face. It burned so much that I soon lost consciousness.

32

COCOONED

I woke up cocooned in spider's silk. My skin felt numb, and I wondered if it was even there. I couldn't feel any sensation in my whiskers, I couldn't smell, I couldn't taste. All I could see was the ground far below me now, lit by the hideous green light from the spider sitting in its web, and the serkets skittering around below it.

The web stretched out in all directions, emanating a slight green, spooky glow. I couldn't see the cocoon I was in, as I couldn't move my head, but I imagined it looked much the same. This stuff was probably eating me alive. Tenderising my skin, perhaps so I'd be tastier for the serkets and the spiders when they decided to feast.

I wanted to shudder, but I couldn't even do that. I knew only one thing, that I was completely and utterly doomed.

I'd been stupid, and I deserved it.

As if the spider had sensed that I'd awoken, it climbed up the web towards me, and then regarded me with its ugly eyes. I could smell something terrible on its breath, and if I could have turned my head away, I would have. But instead, I could only feel sick. But I couldn't even move my diaphragm to throw up.

The spider edged closer to me, and then it let out a shriek, and it raised one of its fangs. I didn't even close my eyes, waiting for the final moment of death to come.

Suddenly, there came a bright blue flash followed by an even more intense white light. I didn't see it directly, only the reflection off the serkets and the spiders. Below me, the serkets screeched out as another orange light filled the cavern. A pleasant warmth arose from somewhere, followed by a loud and bellowing roar.

"Gracious demons, it's a good job we're bonded, otherwise I wouldn't have had a chance of finding you." I couldn't tell you how glad I was to hear Salanraja's voice inside my head. But I was so delirious that I couldn't even put words to thought. Whiskers, I wasn't even sure if what I saw was real, or just some hallucination caused by the spider's poison.

Another blue light streamed through the cavern, this time attached to some kind of glowing ball. This hit me, or at least it hit the cocoon I was entangled in. An intense wave of cold spasmed down my body, as if someone had just thrown me into a bucket of icy water.

Well, it certainly woke me up. *"I'm freezing,"* I said back to Salanraja.

"Good," Salanraja said. *"You deserve a little suffering after what you pulled. You know, when I finally woke, I couldn't reach you for a long time. There was this voice in your head, mumbling something about rabbits over and over again. Then when you started talking about giant scorpions and spiders, I'd pretty much worked out where you'd gone. I don't know if I can forgive you for this, Bengie..."*

"Salanraja..."

But she said nothing else. Instead, another bright orange light came from the entrance, followed by a crackling sound. Then, I heard the frozen web I was in begin to crack. I couldn't feel the venom on my body and leaching into my blood anymore. Instead, I felt strangely refreshed.

The serkets had now turned to face the entrance, gathering in one closely knit crowd. This wasn't the smartest idea, because a wide flame reached out right into the cavern. The walls became laced with terrifying screeches, and the serkets skittered about randomly, many of them turning on their backs with their legs kicking up into the air.

Initiate Rine appeared at the entrance, and he shot out icicles from his staff at some serkets that remained standing. The momentum sent them rolling across the ground as they curled up in balls. Rine sent more icicles after them, pinning them against the wall.

Another human figure then entered the cave but, before I could see who it was, he reached up with his staff and let out these brilliant flashes of light. Yellow and white streaks of lightning shot out from his crystal, connecting one adjacent serket to the next.

If Initiate Rine was powerful, this man was a master. I waited for the light to subside and I only just made out the wrinkles on the familiar face before the cocoon underneath me shattered to pieces.

I hit the ground with a thud, sending up splashes of water from a stream at the bottom of the cave. I rolled over, forgetting that my muscles were still weak and full of poison. I shook off the water in my fur, and then I looked back towards the cave mouth.

Aleam stood there hunched over his staff. He looked left and right across the cavern, assessing the state of a crowd of dying serkets. Many of them had stopped and were motionless. Others still moved their legs, but they did so very slowly, as if on the verge of death.

There came this high-pitched noise like a circular saw grating against metal. A massive shape thudded down in front of me, separating me from Aleam. I was staring right at the massive terrible eyes of that spider, and its huge dripping fangs.

It raised its fangs and charged, shooting a strand of web at me as it did so, as if it was that silly man in the tight red costume the little one liked to watch on TV back in South Wales. I ducked before the web could hit me in the face, and then I dodged under its fangs, trying not to touch that dripping venom.

The spider turned around and reared up on four of its hind legs, as it tried to swipe at me with the front four. I dodged them, hoping that either Rine and Aleam would hurry and work some of their magic on this beast. But I then realised that I might not have that much time. I had to try to take it down by myself.

The spider raised another of its fangs high in the air again, and I waited for the right moment. Just as it came down towards me, I rolled out of the way, and then jumped onto the spider's head. I sprinted across the creature's back, as it screamed and tossed and turned, trying to throw me off. But after those flights Salanraja had taken me on, trying to stay steady on this spider rodeo was nothing in comparison.

That was when I spotted a crystal nestled between two plates at the peak of the spider's bulbous back. It glowed green, much as the rest of the abdomen.

The spider shuddered like an earthquake, sending me tumbling back down its back again. I rolled as if falling down a hill, and I only just caught myself on the chitin of one of the spider's hairy legs. It lifted another leg in front of me and tried to spear me with the single claw at the end of it. But I twisted in the air, and then I pulled myself back onto the back. I ran towards the crystal.

I tried to swipe it out of its socket, but it was a lot harder to dislodge than the crystals in the golem and the Manipulator had been. As the spider was screeched and wriggled underneath me, I suddenly realised that I was backing me into one of its webs.

I had another go with my claw again, trying to get underneath the green crystal. It was wedged between two thick layers of chitin that were pressing against each other like a vice. I tried once more, then I swallowed my fears about swallowing this venom and clasped my teeth around it.

Just as I felt the stickiness of the web against my back, I managed to pry out the crystal. I felt the bitter, rancid taste of spider venom on my tongue, and some wetness trickled down my throat. At the same time, there came a bubbling sound from beneath me, and the venom on the spider's skin boiled as if it were lava. This happened for a few seconds, before the spider exploded, throwing me up into the air together with spatters of green, yucky goo. I yowled out as I hit the wall.

Before I could even turn towards my friends, I was greeted by a grating chittering noise from behind. I could sense the serket right behind me, and I turned to look at its black and lifeless eyes. It had me cornered within a slimy and cold alcove. I tried to scramble up the walls of it, but they were too slippery. There was absolutely no escape.

The serket charged and lunged its stinger forwards. I closed my eyes and prepared to die. What irony – especially right after I'd killed that massive spider.

"Oh no you don't," Ta'ra said from somewhere nearby. The serket hissed, then turned to engage her. It lunged downwards with its sting, but Ta'ra ducked out of the way, shrinking in size as she did. She led the serket away for a moment, then she turned on the charging beast and grew again, until she was three times the size of the arthropod.

Whiskers, she was larger than a lion at this point. She was as large, in fact, as a dragon. The scorpion stuck its sting into her paw, but she looked down at it and yawned. "Is that all you've got, you stupid critter?"

With her other paw, she swiped underneath the serket and knocked it flat on its back. There was something glowing red on its underbelly – another crystal. "You might as well do the honours, Ben," she said. "But be quick, we haven't got all day."

I mewled, and then I ran over. Or more, I should say, I hobbled over. I was still incredibly weak with whiskers knows what chemicals I had inside me. I swiped at the red crystal with my claws. The serket had an unusually soft underbelly, and I managed to knock the crystal away with ease.

The serket lashed at me one more time with its sting, but I was quick enough to get out of the way. Then, it went still, and shrivelled up within its own shell. I looked at Ta'ra, who was now the same size as me, licking the paw the serket had just stung. I mewled once more, and then I rubbed my nose against hers to say thank you.

She laughed. "Flaming demons, Ben," she said. "Why do I have to like you so much?"

The answer to that one was obvious. "Because I'm a Bengal, descendant of the great Asian leopard cat."

"Nah," Ta'ra said with a yawn. "It's just the hormones. I'll get over them in a few days."

She got up and stalked towards the front of the cavern, a certain feline and seductive sway to her hips. As she walked, her back feet landed in the same position as her front feet. She'd clearly been practising.

Initiate Rine and Aleam were busy at the front of the cave mouth knocking the crystals out of the serket's underbellies with the butts of their staffs. Ta'ra went over to help them. I watched them for a moment, thinking that I was too tired to work and that I needed some time to groom myself. But then, I realised that they had come all this way to help me, and I should at least help out a little.

So, I moved towards the front of the cave and helped with the arduous task of knocking the crystals out of the serkets. There were a lot of them, and so it took us an awfully long time.

33

AFTERMATH

I could tell Salanraja was angry, as she'd said nothing to me since my battle with the spider. So, by the time we'd reduced all the serkets to shells on the cave floor, I dreaded going outside.

Aleam, Rine and Ta'ra had already left me there, and I half worried that they might fly off without me. But then, at the same time, I worried that Salanraja would flame me as soon as I left this cave.

After a while, I mustered up the courage to leave. Salanraja had joined a couple of other dragons, each of them feeding upon a carcass of roasted goat. One of these dragons was an emerald with bright red eyes and two charcoal lines of spikes that ran across both flanks. The other was a brilliant white, the colour of snow – and by that I mean proper snow, the type I saw outside the Versta Caverns, and not the yucky type that falls in thin quantities in South Wales once or twice a year.

Both dragons wore saddles and had panniers on either side of them so wide that each bag looked like it could fit a large animal. The humans had created a campfire a little off to the side of the dragons, and they also had another goat roasting on a spit. Really, with all the delicious smells mingling with the air, I should have been starving.

But I don't know if it was because of the spider's poison, or just my general mood, but I'd really lost my appetite.

The sun had set low in the sky, and though that same purple gas was still here, the presence of dragon riders and dragons seemed to push it away. So, the air had a certain freshness to it. Not the kind you'd get in the forest, but it didn't taste stale, at least.

"*So, you finally came out to join us,*" Salanraja said.

"Salanraja," I replied. "*I really don't know what to say. I'm sorry. I shouldn't have run away like that. It was stupid.*"

Salanraja turned to me and snorted. A plume of smoke rose from her nostrils. "*It really was...*"

"*But the warlock,*" I continued. "*Astravar is in my head, and I don't know what to do about him.*" I glanced at the humans and Ta'ra. They hadn't yet seemed to notice that I'd left the caves.

"*I've been keeping Astravar out of your mind, you fool. But if you run away, I won't be able to watch what he's doing in there. Until we find a way to get that crystal you swallowed, Bengie, you need to stay close to me.*"

"*You mean to say that you can protect me from him?*"

"*Usually,*" Salanraja said. "*And I can do it in my sleep as well. It's a by-product of us being bonded – we protect each other. Only once did I let my attention slip. I was so exhausted after battling that bone dragon, I may have let him into your dreams. But as long as I'm close and protecting you, the warlock won't be able to take control.*"

This mind control stuff was so much to take in. Before I'd come to this world, I hadn't even conceived that people could talk to me in this way. It was all rather strange.

"*I'm sorry,*" I said again. "*I really am.*"

A deep rumbling sound came from the base of Salanraja's stomach. "*Just don't do it again. Remember, we're a team, and we need to work together. From now on, you're going to have to accept that.*"

"*Okay,*" I said.

"*Good. Now go and get some food; you really should eat something.*" I looked over at the goats that the dragons were munching into. "*Gracious demons, not here. Go over with the humans. After all we've been through, I don't want to see the other dragons tear you apart.*"

I groaned, and then I pulled myself over to the humans. Each step felt like I was trying to drag my feet through molten lead. My muscles not only ached, but they also burned as if that venom was still raging inside them. I didn't think it would kill me. Luckily, I don't think I'd taken enough of it. But my body still needed to break it down.

I approached the campfire where Initiate Rine and Aleam sat on a long stone ledge jutting out of the crag. Ta'ra sat opposite them, already with a good several scraps of goat in front of her. They must have brought the wood for the fire over in the panniers, because nothing around us looked good for burning.

"*Why don't you get panniers?*" I asked Salanraja.

"*Please shut up,*" Salanraja replied. "*Don't mention that idea to anyone.*"

"*What? Why?*"

"*Because no one who has any power has had that idea yet, and I'd rather fly light, thank you very much. My dragon friends, Ishtkar and Olan here agree it's for the best. If they had any choice, they'd lose the panniers too.*"

I glanced back at the two dragons, who had their heads tucked into their food, without seeming to have a care in the world. "*Which one's which?*" I asked.

"*Ishtkar's the green and Olan's the white. Ishtkar and Rine are bonded, as are Olan and Aleam. Now haven't you got some apologising to do?*"

I meowed, then I jumped up next to Initiate Rine on the ledge. Rine turned to me and turned up his nose. "Come to cause more problems, have you?" he asked. "Because you have no idea how much trouble you almost got me in."

"I came over for…" And I suddenly realised how hungry that the smell of the goat on the spit was making me feel.

"What, you want food now?" Rine said.

"No," I said. "I came to say sorry." Then, I pushed up to him and I let off a soft purr as I sat down next to his hip.

"I guess we're always going to be different," Rine said. "You're a cat, and I'm a human."

"I guess."

Aleam turned to look at me. "You know, Ben. Even if you're new here, you've caused quite a stir at the Council of Three. I'm sorry to say this, but I'm not sure they'll accept you as a dragon rider when we get back. There will be a trial, and the fate for you and Salanraja they were threatening might come to pass."

"But it was me who stepped out of line," I pointed out. "She doesn't deserve to get punished for it." Whiskers, no wonder she was angry with me.

"It doesn't matter," Aleam said. "You're bonded and your responsibility is also Salanraja's. You get rewarded together for your good deeds, and you get punished together for your bad. That is the law."

"Not just that," Rine said as he tore a thick strand of meat off a bone. "But you got me into trouble too. There's a reason why I brought Ishtkar out here. Fortunately, Driar Aleam had the heart to help too, because I'm not sure I could have handled these creatures alone."

"And me," Ta'ra said, and slinked around the fire. "Don't forget about me." She jumped up and sat on Aleam's lap.

"You were the bravest of all, Ta'ra," Aleam said with a chuckle, and I don't know why, but something about that was funny. I couldn't help but laugh. Like a human…

34

AN EPIPHANY

After we'd all eaten and had some time to chat the evening away, Initiate Rine and Aleam put out the fire then strapped up the panniers and tightened the saddles on the dragons. I had remained silent through the rest of the meal, as I kind of realised that I had an ordeal ahead of me. I felt awful, I really did. Both Salanraja and I would be punished, me probably locked up in the cattery and not even let out on rat duty in case I ever tried running away again.

Meanwhile, I couldn't imagine what they might do to Salanraja. They might clip her wings or something, which is what I heard they did to those nasty swan birds that every cat but Adam knew not to go anywhere near.

There was also something else bothering me. I remembered that conversation that High Prefect Lars had had with his friend, Asinda in the dining hall. He'd mentioned something about a demon dragon.

I walked over to Aleam as he tightened the straps on Olan's saddle to try and find out some more. "Aleam," I said. "Can I ask you something?"

Aleam turned to me and raised an eyebrow. "Go on…"

"I heard about the demon dragon," I said. "High Prefect Lars was talking about it in the dining room."

"Terrible thing," Aleam said, shaking his head. "I just hope the king can send enough forces in time to stop it. Otherwise, no dragon rider or mage on this world will be able to kill it. It will hunt all dragons down and then it will destroy cities, and after a year there might be nothing left of civilisation on this world."

I thought about it a moment. Then, I remembered what the crystal had shown me. How South Wales had become a barren landscape, my owners lying down as skeletons on the master bed. Could it be the demon dragon that caused this? All because of the demon rats I killed...

"How long until he summons it?" I asked.

"The problem is that we don't know," Aleam replied. "Nor do we know exactly where the warlocks will perform the ceremony, or which warlock will be involved."

"Astravar..." I said.

"How do you know?"

"He told me his plans in a dream," he said. "And he wants me to be part of them."

"If only we knew where he was," Aleam replied. "Then maybe we could put a stop to this. We have scouts out hunting the Darklands for him. But I fear we don't have enough time."

I left Aleam to finish checking the saddle on his dragon, feeling as if I'd failed everyone. If I hadn't come to this world, none of this might have happened. But I was just part of Astravar's nefarious plans.

That was when I felt a force in my head. It felt as if there was a stone just behind my nose, and someone was pulling it gently. A sudden image entered my mind. I saw Astravar in the middle of a massive pentagram, set in the centre of a shallow crater in the grey earth. He had tiny bodies arranged all around him – the husks of dead rats. He stared right into a crystal on a pedestal, which fed light into a massive hole in the sky. This shimmered like the surface of a lake, reflecting the putrid landscape that surrounded the warlock.

Suddenly, he turned his head as if he knew I was watching him, and I batted my eyelids and blinked him away.

I turned around to see that Initiate Rine and Aleam had already mounted. Ta'ra was sat on Aleam's lap, strapped into a belt that the old man had wrapped around his legs.

"*Come on, little one,*" Salanraja said. "*It's time to face our punishment.*"

"*Wait,*" I replied and I sprinted right past Salanraja and then in front of the emerald and the white dragon. They had their legs lowered, as if they were ready to take off. "Wait!" I shouted out loud.

Rine pulled on the reins in front of me and then looked down from his dragon. "What is it now?" he called back.

"It's Astravar. He's starting to perform the ceremony to summon the demon dragon, and I know exactly where he is."

35

FLIGHT TO ASTRAVAR

After I'd delivered my news that I knew where Astravar was, Initiate Rine and Aleam had told me not to be fanciful, and Salanraja had called me an idiot inside my head. But I informed them that since I'd swallowed the golem's gemstone, somehow it worked as a compass between me and the warlock. That caused them to become more interested. Aleam put his hand to his chin, scratching it, then he gazed off towards the purple horizon.

"We should go," he said. "I think the young cat is right." Aleam also instructed his dragon to call for reinforcements from Dragonsbond Academy. But he didn't think they'd get there in time to stop Astravar summoning the demon dragon. We had the advantage of distance, and so it was down to us.

Hence, we took off into the sky.

We had a long flight ahead of us, through the Wastelands and into the Darklands. Fortunately, we took a sharp right at some point, as we wanted to minimise the encounters with griffins and harpies and other horrible minions of the warlocks that I couldn't remember the names of.

I'd been tripping out on those purple gases so long, that the green and the yellow hues of Illumine's fields didn't look so vivid and straight as they should. Rather, they spun by below, whirling and dancing in my vision, as if they were alive. Though, this might have been a side effect of the venom, admittedly.

After a while the effect wore off. The air tasted fresh again. The grey layer of clouds had lifted by this point, and the sun had passed through, casting its warm rays upon the farmers and sheep down below. It also helped allay the effect of the strong and cold wind, somewhat.

We passed by Midar village, and I looked down at the sheep pen. The young lady – Rala the shepherdess – was down there shearing the wool off her flock of six sheep. She turned up to look at us, shielding her eyes as we passed.

After that, the sun set, and we flew under the cover of night without stopping. As we progressed, the weather got colder, and the air took on a smell of rotten eggs. We didn't have time for camping. Astravar could complete the ceremony at any time.

I was still worried. This could easily be another trap. Astravar could have faked my visions for all I knew. Maybe the portal wasn't to summon a demon dragon, but to suck us all into the Seventh Dimension. Then, from what Salanraja had told me, we'd have to deal with demon beasts of all kinds.

"We're all fully aware of what we might be flying into," Salanraja told me. *"But we don't have time to wait for reinforcements to arrive. Nothing can kill a demon dragon once it's out of the Seventh Dimension. If Astravar succeeds in summoning it, it will eliminate anything that we send at it and eventually destroy everything upon this world."*

I guess she was right, but I couldn't help but shudder at the thought of a massive invulnerable dragon from another dimension. Whiskers, Salanraja was scary enough.

The thought of it all made my skin itchy, and the only way to calm the stress was to groom myself with my paws and tongue. But then I recalled that I had just been wrapped in a venomous cobweb, and so licking myself didn't seem such a good idea.

We turned back into the Wastelands, just as day approached. There was a beautiful sunrise that brought farmers out from their huts to watch. The massive orb in the sky cast brilliant red rays over the fields, and it made me feel good to be alive.

"This is the best part of flying," Salanraja said. *"To experience sights like these."*

But unfortunately, this sight was short-lived, because that odorous purple horizon was approaching and the mist there was thicker than I'd seen it before. We soon hit it like one hits a wall, and with it an intense chill washed over me. That dense purple fog had taken over the land and sky, and I imagined how a massive demon dragon might jump out of the murk and swat us down in one fell swoop.

I felt a sense of emptiness from the absence of the sunrise. Everything that I'd lived for, the good life full of milk and salmon trimmings for breakfast in the morning, running over my owners' lawn in South Wales trying to bat the butterflies out of the air. All this, I'd now had to leave behind so I could face my destiny.

"Do you have to be so melodramatic?" Salanraja said. *"I think I prefer the old Bengie."*

"Well he's gone," I said, clenching my jaw. *"This time, we're going to stop that evil warlock and then you and I will force him to send me back through the portal."*

A slow and sonorous rumbling came from Salanraja's chest underfoot. *"Do you really want to go home? Does our bond matter to you so little?"*

I hesitated as I lowered my head. Of course, the bond was important to me. But then, I didn't ask for any of this.

"I don't know," I replied. *"Let's just take this one step at a time."*

The mist soon cleared a little, and I could make out some shapes through the murk. There was a tall tower there, which I presumed to be Astravar's. It's funny, when I was running away from it, I never turned around to look at it. But now, I could see how menacing the thing looked. With the mist drifting around it, it looked almost like a ghost flickering in and out of existence. On the top of it, it had what looked like a raised crown, with thorns like spades sticking out the top instead of parapets.

Seeing it now, part of me wondered if I could just summon the portal myself. Maybe I could just climb off Salanraja, run to the top of

Astravar's tower that would be conveniently unlocked for me and then step into the centre of his portal. Shazam, it would open up for me, and the next moment I'll be looking right into my bowl of milk and salmon trimmings. None of this would have happened and everything could go back to normal.

But then, such a portal could take me to the dangerous Savannah. A land full of hippopotamuses that would tear me up with their razor-sharp buck teeth or take me down underneath the mud and suffocate me. The worst deaths, I had heard, happened underneath the belly of the hippopotamus. Oh, those Savannah cats were such storytellers.

"Will you stop daydreaming your nonsense," Salanraja said. *"We're almost there."*

I'd been in such a reverie, I'd lost track of what was going on around us. We'd taken a sharp turn away from the tower and were now heading towards a shallow mountain range.

"There," I heard Initiate Rine call out from Ishtkar's back on my right. He pointed off into the distance with his staff.

I looked where he was pointing, at a white glow coming up from the horizon. "Is that it?" I called out, struggling to raise my voice over the loudness of the wind.

"Yes," Salanraja replied. *"Now brace yourself. It's now time to find out what that warlock has in store."*

36

BONE DRAGON BATTLE

W e saw the bone dragons first, and this time we didn't have only one to contend with but a good dozen of them. They were wheeling around in a circle above the ground created from the dried husks of all the demon rats I'd killed. There must have been thousands of them – I never realised I'd killed so many. That then made me wonder how much of my stay in Astravar's tower I remembered. Maybe the warlock hadn't needed me to swallow the golem's crystal for him to take control of my mind. Maybe he'd had dominion over me all along.

Manipulators stood outside of the circle feeding energy into the bone dragons. Each had a dragon of their own, and they slithered around on the ground as they tracked the position of their minions.

Astravar stood in the centre of the circle, with a crystal on a pedestal in front of him. He was bent over this with his arms stretched out wide, and his lips were moving as if chanting a ritual. But we were too far away to hear what he was saying.

The crystal cast a bright light out from the circle, almost as bright as the sun had been before. It seemed to be feeding its energy into a massive oval as tall as a castle. It shimmered white around the edges, and the reflection of our world faded, to display a land full of fire and magma. The Seventh Dimension. It couldn't be anything else.

There was also something standing next to Astravar, that looked rather feline and slightly overweight. It had red skin, with cracks running down it that looked like they were on fire. Black smoke rose from the beast as it stared up at me with red glowing eyes, as if challenging me to come down and fight it. As Salanraja got closer, I also saw the thing was massive, perhaps four times the size of me. But we were moving so fast I couldn't quite make out what it was.

My major concern wasn't the massive beast or the massive portal thingy, anyway. It was the bone dragons that screeched up into the air in unison, and then wheeled around in the sky to face us. One of them was coming at Salanraja head on.

"Hold on..." Salanraja called out in my mind.

"You keep saying that when I've got nothing to hold on t—"

Before I knew it, purple flame was spewing out of the bone dragon's mouth. Some of it brushed against my fur, withering it on touch. Presently, Salanraja performed a barrel roll and swooped out of the way, sending me spinning around in her second rib cage again. All this time, when I'd stood in front of the washing machine in South Wales, watching clothes spin round and round, I never thought I'd end up in one. But at that moment, I couldn't help but feel sorry for the clothes.

I scrambled up Salanraja's back to stop myself falling off. I reached the top just as Salanraja reached her apex, and all seemed still for a moment. I caught sight of Aleam and Rine flying side by side on their dragons. They had their staffs stuck out in front of them as they headed towards two bone dragons while another three chased them on their tails. Flashes of lightning came out of Aleam's staff, while Rine tossed out a stream of water that quickly froze and then shattered in the air.

But they only knocked the bone dragons out of the way, which soon corrected themselves and flew back off into the distance, ready to strike again.

Salanraja started to climb again, and I ran back up to her neck, doing everything I could to stay there without falling off. I turned to see that we had another two bone dragons on our tail, but Salanraja veered quickly to the right, to throw them off target.

"What are we going to do, Salanraja?" I asked, as the turning force pushed me into one side of her corridor of spikes.

I felt Salanraja's back muscles tense underneath my skin. *"I've already talked to the other dragons about it, who of course have discussed this with their riders."*

"And their conclusion is?"

Another roar came from behind and some purple flame swooped over my head. It wasn't hot, but rather felt like a spray of concentrated acid. Some of it touched the back of my ears, and it really stung.

Salanraja executed a loop-the-loop, and I cursed as I thought I'd fall right out of the sky. She got on top of the bone dragon that had assailed us, and as I lay on my back pressed against the top of Salanraja's second ribcage, I wanted to throw up. Then, she came back down, so she was behind the thing, and she opened her mouth and let out a loud roar mixed with a jet of fire. Of course, it didn't do much damage.

In a way, I didn't see much point in fighting these things if they couldn't be defeated without first destroying their Manipulators. But I guess dragons and dragon riders enjoyed making pretty patterns in the sky with their magic.

"Just get down on the ground, and fight," Salanraja said. *"We need Aleam's and Rine's magic up here to fight the bone dragons."*

Memories of the battle with the previous bone dragon flashed across my mind. I remembered the thorns, and the sting, and almost dying in my sleep. *"I can't take all the Manipulators,"* I pointed out.

"No, don't stop them. Stop Astravar's ceremony. Winning this battle is much more important than our own lives."

Salanraja dived towards the ground, and she jerked into a hover, throwing me towards her tail. Instead of trying to grasp on for my dear life, I submitted and let myself roll down it. I landed on the cold and dusty ground.

I lifted myself up to see that massive beast standing right before me. It opened its mouth and let out a terrible hiss as it displayed a fine set of incredibly sharp teeth.

37

MEET THY NEMESIS

I couldn't believe what I was looking at. I had never seen one in my life before, even if I knew them to be the king of domesticated cats. I scanned the cavernous, pointed ears that rose high above its head, its menacing glowing eyes set into a flat face, and a mane and beard that extended far below its chin.

It was massive. It was hideous.

I was standing face to face with a Maine Coon. Except this wasn't a normal Maine Coon, it was a demon Maine Coon, presumably summoned from the Seventh Dimension. So maybe I hadn't killed as many demon rats as I thought, because this thing looked like it would be great at killing things. Forget about the demon dragon. With this thing at Astravar's disposal, every cat in this land was doomed.

I could feel the heat coming off of it, as if I was facing a pile of burning embers. If not for the fiery cracks in its skin, the beast would have been a flat charcoal colour. It was also big – I hadn't gathered the true scale of it from the air. But it was certainly bigger than a lion. Perhaps it was even bigger than Ta'ra had been when she'd knocked the senses out of that serket.

Whiskers, why wasn't she down here instead of me? Surely that would have been a fairer fight. I glanced upwards to try and catch sight of the Cat Sidhe on the white dragon. But I couldn't see her and Olan now had four bone dragons on its tail.

The demon cat opened its mouth and yawned. Red slaver run out from its mouth and fell towards the ground. This sizzled when it hit the rock, leaving a black char mark. Around it, the purple gas danced and swayed, and I noticed then that the cat's eyes weren't just glowing. They were like windows looking into a raging furnace inside the Maine Coon's head, as if fire had replaced its brain.

"NO CAT CAN DEFEAT HELLCAT," it said incredibly loudly, hissing out the cat language that I'd not heard for so long.

It arched its back and circled me, and I followed its path, wondering how I had any chance of taking this thing down. I tried to see behind it, so I could ascertain the position of the crystal. But my enemy blocked any possible path I had through.

So, I arched my back just like him, and hissed back at him. I don't know what I was thinking, really. It was just natural instinct kicking in, really. But there was another feeling in my gut that was telling me to run, Ben. Get as far from this place as I could and leave the fate of the world in the dragons' and the dragon riders' hands.

A roar came from the sky, just as the demon cat crouched down and then leaped at me. I rolled out of the way, feeling the heat from it searing against me. Whiskers, I really didn't want to touch that thing. But it was quick to turn around, and I was soon facing it again. I thought of charging for the crystal, but I had no time before it pounced again. I lifted myself on my hind paws to parry the blow. It was stupid, because the demon cat caught me by the shoulders and pinned me to the ground.

I wriggled and tried to free myself from the demon's grasp. My shoulders burned as if I was pinned underneath two red-hot iron pokers. I wanted to cry out in pain, but it was too much for me to even move my mouth. I struggled, and I gasped for breath, and I thought I was going to pass out.

That's when the Maine Coon suddenly rolled off me along the ground. Salanraja's skin brushed against my legs, and she took back off into the air. I stood up, and I finally took an opportunity to yowl out my pain.

"You can't kill it, Ben," Salanraja said. *"Don't even try. Go for the crystal!"*

The demon Maine Coon lifted itself up and spun around to face me again. It opened its mouth and hissed and growled as it looked up at Salanraja, who was now doing a loop-the-loop to avoid a purple flame coming from a bone dragon approaching from her side.

"The crystal, Ben!" Salanraja said.

I turned and looked at the pedestal. Astravar was facing away from me, his arms now stretched above his head. I heard the demon cat scuff the ground behind me, and I took the opportunity to run. I sprinted faster than a greyhound chasing after a lump of steak. Or at least that's how it seemed at the time.

But the massive demon cat was close on my tail, and I had to dodge to the right to stop it barrelling into me and pinning me back to the ground. I felt the heat from it as it brushed against me, but I had too much adrenaline in me, which propelled me forwards towards my target.

There it was, in front of me, so much white light glowing from the crystal that it almost blinded me. I leapt up onto the pedestal, and I heard Astravar shout out from behind me.

"You!" he screamed.

But he was too late, because I readied a huge swipe and I knocked at the crystal with all my might. It was much steadier on its perch than it looked, and the impact sent a shudder up my paw to my shoulder that was already screaming at me from the burn. So, I used more strength than a cat could possibly have to push the heavy crystal towards the edge, putting my head, shoulder, and back into it. Eventually, it toppled to the floor, making a loud crashing sound.

It shattered, sending up shards of whatever it was made of into the air and filling the sky with a prismatic display of light.

"You did it, Bengie," Salanraja said, and there came a great bellowing from the sky. The victory cries of not one dragon, but three.

But that's when I noticed something was wrong. Because Astravar was nowhere to be seen, and the demon Maine Coon was sprinting to a point where a bright white light shone out of the horizon. Around me, the circle of dead demon rats had completely disappeared off the ground.

38

OUT OF THE PORTAL

T he Manipulators tossed their wispy heads into the sky, looking like they wanted to scream out. But they were silent, as their energy leeched out of them, and dissipated into the earth. The bone dragons also withered away in the sky, turning into flakes of what looked like black charcoal. Surprisingly, no crystals dropped out of them, nor did any crystals fall from the Manipulators onto the ground.

The portal had completely vanished as well, almost as if it had never been there at all.

"Gracious demons," Salanraja said. *"We've been tricked."*

"What, how?"

"That crystal you knocked out was only summoning an illusion. No time to explain. Follow now!"

Above, Olan was already heading towards that glowing spot on the horizon, and Ishtkar and Salanraja wheeled around in the sky and dived, using gravity to their advantage to catch up with the white dragon. I groaned from deep inside the belly, part of me wanting to turn around and go back to being wild again.

But we all know how that turned out last time. I needed to help my friends.

I could still see the demon Maine Coon, and so I summoned up some remaining threads of energy and sprinted right after him. My legs felt like jelly at first, and my body really wanted to give up. I panted as I went, and I pushed myself so hard that all of my muscles burned.

I arrived at a circle made of the same demon rats that I'd seen before. In fact, everything looked so similar that I realised what I'd just battled must have been a mirror duplicate of this scene. Except that there were no Manipulators. It was just Astravar and the demon Maine Coon.

There was also a massive white portal, just like the first one. Except it now had a fiery red centre to it, which rippled as I moved. It looked almost as if I was staring through a pool of water into another world. Which, in retrospect, I guess I was.

Astravar had a staff in his hand with a dark purple crystal set into the head of it. He pointed this at the crystal on the pedestal, feeding it with purple energy, which turned into white energy that fed the portal proper.

The dragons swooped down as one and tried to flame Astravar. But he just raised his staff into the air and swept it from the floor over his head in one fluid motion. A purple barrier of light blossomed out of him, and the flames met that and didn't go any further. The dragons continued their dive, and they hit the barrier head on. They ended up bouncing off it, and all three of them struggled to recover in the sky.

Whiskers, I don't know how the dragon riders managed to stay on their mounts. But then, I guess they had the luxury of being strapped into their saddles.

As the dragons swept around for another pass, Astravar's voice boomed out so loudly that I thought he had one of those funny shaped devices that humans used in carnivals and the like to amplify their voice. "You are too late," he said. "The ritual is complete, and the world will soon belong to us."

That was when there came an intense flash of red light from the portal. It felt like the entire world burned with flame for just a moment, and I thought I was going to get scorched alive. Then, the ground shook underfoot, and a roar ten times louder than thunder filled the sky.

It all happened in less than a second, after which the red light faded, and there was the demon dragon flying out of the portal from its previous world.

It was five times the size of the dragons and had those same cracks in its skin that I'd seen on the demon Maine Coon's body. The air around it seemed to shimmer, almost as if it was getting sucked into what burned beneath the demon dragon.

"*No!*" Salanraja screamed out in my head.

The dragons had turned around to face the demon, and they were already charging in once again. But the mighty demon dragon opened its mouth, and the ground trembled so violently I was knocked off of my feet. A spherical pulse of energy shot out of the dragon, looking very much like the surface of a bubble lined with veins of fire. Salanraja, Olan, and Ishtkar flew right into it, and then the energy field swept them away.

It was as if they'd just been hit by a cricket bat the size of a cloud, and soon, all three dragons became lost to sight.

A voice thundered out, so deep it sounded like that man who played the father lion in that cartoon the kid in South Wales used to love to watch. "I AM DEMON DRAGON," it bellowed. "CONJURATION OF THE WARLOCK ASTRAVAR. THIS WORLD SHALL SOON BE HIS."

A little voice inside me wanted to call back, "Big deal, I'm a Bengal, descendant of the great Asian leopard cat." But an even bigger voice told me that this creature probably wouldn't be so impressed.

The demon dragon flew off in the direction it had knocked the other three dragons. It wasn't travelling particularly fast, I noticed. But then it was a great lumbering beast.

I turned to Astravar, now looking down on me with his pale face and lifeless grey eyes. Like in my dream, his skin had taken on a certain blueness and had started to crack a little like an eggshell. This dark magic addiction was changing him in most unnatural ways.

I wanted to approach Astravar and at least scratch him with my long claws and show him how much I hated him. I took a step forward, but his pet demon Maine Coon, my replacement, blocked my path. It raised its back and hissed at me.

Astravar looked down at him and laughed. "Cats will always be cats," he said. "No matter what realm I summon them from."

"And humans will always be humans," I replied. "Who are meant to live in servitude of cats."

"Not in this world," Astravar replied. "Although, it would seem that if I let it have its way, then humans would eventually let that happen. But they will never have a chance. Once this world is my own, I shall seize control of all dimensions. I don't need the other warlocks now. I can do this alone."

I growled at him. "What do you want of me, Astravar?" I said. "I had a good life, and you had to bring me here. You deserve to die."

"Maybe I will one day," Astravar said with a grin that chapped his lips, "and then I shall come back a greater being. I thought of doing the same to you. But I'm not sure you deserve it anymore. It's a shame. I brought you here thinking you might be interested in becoming one of the most powerful beings across the dimensions. But it looks like you're not as opportunistic as I first thought."

"I just want to live my life," I said. "Eating and sleeping and grooming and playing..."

"No, you don't. You want to survive like any creature upon this world. But that's the irony of it all, you have never been powerful enough to survive alone. Just like the humans... Or at least the ones who don't claim power for themselves." He pointed his staff in my direction, and he shot a bolt of purple energy out of it. The beam hit the ground right next to me and caused a rock there to shatter into pieces. Astravar curled up his mouth and laughed, entertained by his cruelty.

He was a bad man that one, of the kind that liked to tease and torture cats.

I stared back at him, licking my lips. If he was going to kill me, he might as well do it here and now. At least I wouldn't have to deal with this world anymore, and I wouldn't have to witness the destruction of all the wonderful food within it.

The warlock sighed wistfully, and then he jumped on the demon Maine Coon. I couldn't help but hope that doing so gave him a burnt bottom. He pointed his staff off into the distance.

But before he had gone far, he stopped the Maine Coon, and he twisted around and let off another bolt of purple energy. This fizzled as it hit the ground next to me, and sparks flew out from the impact point in all directions. These created more impact points, and the ground seemed to melt for a moment. Then, red sprouts shot out of it in all directions, and out of these grew hideous thorns and those snapping heads that I'd had to deal with during my first encounter with a Manipulator.

Astravar's voice boomed out once again.

"This world will teach you, Dragoncat, how you are truly incapable of survival," and he rode off into the distance, his maniacal laughter trailing in his wake.

39

TOSS UP

The forest of Mandragoras grew and grew, and the thorns became thicker and thicker. Their heads snapped into the air as if feeding on a flock of sparrows. Everywhere I looked, I could see thickening stems and thorns that I knew were tipped with venom. I couldn't see any way out.

Astravar had kindly left a large circle around me that kept me safe from this forest. But it was slowly closing in on me, as the plants continued to grow on their own accord. I could try running through. But I'd get stung so many times, it would kill me.

"*Salanraja,*" I called out in my mind. "*Salanraja, are you out there?*"

I heard no reply, and I could only assume her to be unconscious. She'd probably been stupid enough to fight the demon dragon, even though she knew she couldn't kill it.

I tried to find a path through the plants. I saw a glimmer in the distance between the thorns, indicating sky. I was probably going to die anyway, so I might as well try something.

That's when I noticed the purple mist creeping in from the outside. It was getting thicker, and as it moved more and more stems seemed to grow out of it. It was as if the mist fed the plants and gave them life.

I stood meowing from the back of my throat and feeling hopeless. The gas soon reached me, and I found myself unable to breathe. I was weak, and I fell down on the ground, my legs collapsing under me. Thorns writhed above me, and my vision went red and blurry.

A roar came out from the distance, faint now, but still like thunder. I knew what it was, the demon dragon creating even more carnage.

"*Salanraja*," I cried out again. "*Please, I need you.*"

Her voice came back to me faint. "*Hold on, Bengie. Hang in there...*"

"*Salanraja... I can't breathe.*"

"*Just one more moment...*"

The branches of these terrible plants were now almost close enough to touch me. They didn't seem to want to lash out like before, as if they knew that I was rendered helpless and there was no point in spending energy on sudden movements. I closed my eyes, ready for them to pierce my skin and inject their deadly poisons into me.

But then, strong claws grappled around my waist, and lifted me up into the sky. I opened my eyes, wondering if this was one of those angel creatures that sent you up to cat heaven. In that place, our old Ragamuffin mentor had said, you could have as much salmon and chicken liver as you wanted. Apparently, angel cats had wings, but I don't think they had long scaly talons like the ones that were gripped around me.

I came to my senses pretty quickly. "*Salanraja you came*," I said, my eyes a little bleary.

"*Of course*," she replied. "*We're bonded, and I won't let you die. Now get up onto my back.*"

"*I—*" But I didn't have a chance to even start my thought, because Salanraja shot suddenly upwards. She gained momentum, so she could open her claws, tossing me out of them. I rose, and then I started to fall, looking down at the forest of those terrible thorny plants and purple gas that had formed around them.

I plummeted, and I shrieked out into the wind, although I'm sure nothing heard me. I landed on Salanraja's back and tumbled down her corridor of spikes before I caught myself on one outer rib with my claws. I lifted myself up to safety, then I sat down, breathing heavily.

I couldn't believe it. I was alive. But I felt sick...

So, I threw up on Salanraja's back.

"What in the Seventh Dimension?"

"I couldn't help it," I replied. *"And it's me who should be complaining. You almost killed me."*

"What? I saved your life, and then you thank me with the contents of your stomach for it."

I growled. *"Just never do that again."*

"Fine, I'll abandon you in the warlock's forest next time."

"Not that. Never toss me up in the air and catch me like that again. What if I'd hit the ground?"

"Bengie, we haven't any time for your moaning right now. We need to meet up with our friends."

She turned sharply in the air, and I watched the forest disappear below. It wasn't long before we broke out into Illumine again, and I breathed the fresh air as if I'd just emerged from my mother's womb and was tasting it for the first time.

40

SO MANY WASTED FISH

S alanraja didn't seem to want to take time to slow down and appreciate the scenery. We flew over a forest – this time a normal one with pine trees in it. There was a glade down there, with a long blue lake that stretched across it. We approached a silver beach where Olan and Ishtkar were waiting. Salanraja landed so heavily on it, that I ended up tumbling off her back onto the sand.

"Ben," I heard Aleam say. He was there in the distance, setting up a load of fish bones in a circle. In the centre of this there was a wooden pedestal, with a massive crystal on it just like the one Astravar had used to summon the dragon.

I soon spotted Rine and Ta'ra out on a small raft on the lake. Rine had a rod raised over the water whilst Ta'ra was crouched over the side of the raft, her head lowered to the surface as her head rolled from side to side.

I jumped up from the sand, forgetting about the injuries from my scrap with the Demon Maine Coon. I moved over to Aleam, purring, and I rubbed my cheek against his knee. "Please let it be salmon," I said. "Finally, are you about to find salmon?"

Aleam didn't turn to me, as he continued to concentrate on getting the exact arrangement of fish bones. I didn't like being ignored, so I moved over to one of the bones right next to him and knocked it out of the way.

"Don't do that," he said. "We must get it in exactly the right position."

"But it's fish. I've not tasted salmon in ages."

"Just…" Aleam shook his head. "This is much more important than your stomach. We've found a lake abundant in fish, and we're using their bones to summon up an offering to the Seventh Dimension. I'll need to concentrate, because I don't want to have to deal with a demon tetrapod as well as a demon dragon."

I blinked at him. "A what?"

"An ancient demon fish," Aleam said. "Now, let me get back to my work."

I growled, and I moved over to the water, watching as Rine and Ta'ra lifted fish after fish from the water. As they did, I wondered which ones would be salmon and which ones wouldn't. Come to think of it, I had absolutely no idea what salmon looked like in the wild. The fish they lifted out seemed rather small, and I'd heard from the Savannah cats that a salmon could be as large as an Asian leopard cat. Which meant they had to be massive.

"Don't you want to know what Aleam is doing?" Salanraja asked me.

I yawned. "I guess you're going to tell me, anyway?"

"Of course. We don't have a chance of killing the demon dragon. But we might be able to lure it back. If we can trick it back to where it came from, then we only need to close the portal."

"What? That's a suicide mission!"

"If we don't," Salanraja said. "Then it will kill us eventually, whether we like it or not. That beast has only one purpose, to destroy any mortal life it finds. Or at least that is the task Astravar has set for it."

I crouched down in the sand and gazed out into the distance. Rine and Ta'ra had gathered a sackful of fish, and Rine was rowing the raft back towards shore. "How does Aleam know how to do this stuff, anyway? Is he some kind of warlock himself?"

"*Kind of,*" Salanraja replied, and she lowered her head to the ground and looked at me with her yellow eyes. I turned to meet her gaze, now not at all scared of her massive head. "*Several years ago, King Garmin of Illumine Kingdom decided that he wanted to train up eight powerful mages to help protect the kingdom from its enemies in other lands. Use of dark crystals for magic had been banned by his ancestors long before him. But he decided to bring their use into the realm. Aleam was one of those mages, and the others became the seven warlocks.*"

"*You mean to say the other seven turned on the king?*"

"Yes," Salanraja replied. "*The power in dark crystals corrupts the mind of those that use it, just as the power in the light crystals brings them closer to their souls. But dragon riders are immune to the effect dark magic has on the mind. It is we dragons who protect you from the darkness that seeks to taint your souls, which is how I managed to keep Astravar out of yours – most of the time, anyway.*"

"*So, what you're saying is that Aleam could have turned out just like the other warlocks?*"

"*Exactly. If he hadn't found Olan and bonded with him, then he probably would have. Dark magic is now once again banned within the Kingdom of Illumine. But the warlocks betrayed King Garmin long ago and tore apart a large part of his kingdom which they claimed as their own. This was the Darklands. Soon after, the Wastelands became a battlefield, where the king's Mages of the Light fought against the warlocks, each trying to gain power for themselves.*"

"*But what does this magic from crystals of the light do, exactly?*" I asked.

"*Not much that's useful in war, unfortunately. It helps build cities and wealth and heal those in need. It's focused on growth, whilst the warlock's magic is focused on decay.*"

Rine and Ta'ra had almost reached the shore now. Rine lowered his oar down into the sand and pulled the raft in. I looked in awe at the massive sack they had on that boat, imagining its tasty contents. The bag was literally wriggling, with all those poor fish inside trying to escape. Perhaps I should have felt sorry for them, but I was too hungry to care.

Rine hefted up the sack and lugged it onto shore. He placed it just outside the circle that Aleam had created, but he didn't open it. Rine turned to Aleam, then he lifted up his staff off his back. Aleam did the same.

"Are you ready?" Rine asked.

"Yes," Aleam said.

I was already at the sack, sniffing at its contents, relishing the smell of something I'd not eaten for so long.

"Stand back," Rine said. "Unless you want to be a fried cat."

I didn't need to be warned twice. I dashed out of the way and then turned around to see what the humans were up to. A massive bolt of blue shot out of Rine's staff. It hit the sack in the centre and immediately froze the material on the outside. Then, Aleam took his turn to send out a cascade of yellow lightning. His magic hit the sack and then the sparks danced over its surface, as Rine added more and more of his ice to the recipe.

"What are you doing?" I cried out. "Stop, you'll waste all that lovely food."

"Oh, can't you stop worrying about your stomach all the time," Ta'ra said, stepping up to me. "We've got a demon dragon to stop."

"But the food," I protested, and I watched with wide eyes as the sack shrunk under the power that Aleam and Rine fed into it. My heart sank in my chest, and I realised that I wouldn't be getting any salmon today.

After a while, the sack tore apart and shrivelled under the forces that Rine and Aleam were putting upon it. Fish bone after fish bone tumbled out of it, all of them devoid of flesh.

"That should be enough," Aleam said. "Now, it's time to get on with your duties, Rine. Ben, you and Salanraja shall accompany him."

I wasn't listening. I was just staring in shock at the smouldering pile of fish bones that didn't even smell like fish anymore.

"*Ben, will you stop being so selfish for once?*" Salanraja requested. "*And jump on my back.*"

"*But why do you need me there?*" I said. "*What use am I going to be against a demon dragon?*"

"Just get on," Salanraja said, and she fixed a stern gaze upon me. Ta'ra was staring at me too, looking at me in a cat's expression of what I could only describe as disappointment. For some reason, I didn't want to let her down.

"Fine," I said out loud, and I turned and ran up Salanraja's tail. She took us up, up, and away in pursuit of the demon dragon.

41

THE DEMON DRAGON

Rine was soon flying alongside us on Ishtkar's back. Aleam, Olan and Ta'ra meanwhile stayed on the ground. From up high, I watched Ta'ra help lift the fish bones with her mouth and drop them in the right position. Aleam had them all neatly arranged, and from this height it all looked like an intricate clock pattern. The wind was warm, but this soon chilled as we gained altitude.

"*Why does she get to stay?*" I asked Salanraja, as I felt a little jealous for the fact she could wrap her mouth around the fishbones and get a slight taste of them, even if Rine and Aleam had completely destroyed the food.

"*Because she isn't bonded to a dragon,*" Salanraja replied. "*And you are.*"

"*But I still don't understand what use I can be up here. I can't shoot jets of ice like Rine can. I don't have any of that useful battle magic.*"

"*Do you know how to summon a portal?*"

"*No...*"

"*Then even the tiniest use you can be up here,*" Salanraja said, "*is better than making mischief on the ground.*"

She had a point, I guess. The demon dragon was flying slowly, and Salanraja and Ishtkar seemed to be putting all their strength into catching up with it.

This, we soon did. I saw the air shimmering on the horizon before I saw the great lumbering beast. Black smoke drifted up from the huge rents in its skin and trailed behind it in the sky. It didn't seem threatened by our arrival and didn't turn to knock us out of the sky. It just carried on its path, as if no force upon this world could stop it.

"*What do we do now?*" I asked Salanraja.

"*Well, we've not quite worked that one out yet.*"

I felt the hackles shoot up on my back. "*You've not worked it out? I thought you said that Aleam had it all planned out.*"

"*We had up to the how do you make a demon dragon turn around, bit.*" Salanraja said. "*Now, all we have to do is annoy it so much that it abandons its orders to destroy Dragonsbond Academy and instead comes chasing after us.*"

"*And how do we do that?*"

"*We try everything we can, and we don't give up,*" Salanraja replied.

Great, I thought. I'd never even imagined such idiocy would be possible.

"*I heard that.*"

"*Good,*" I said.

Beside me, Ishtkar let out a massive roar and sprayed fire out of his muzzle. Salanraja joined in the battle cry, and they were both casting amber jets of flame at the demon dragon, as if trying to set something on fire that was already on fire. See what I mean by idiocy.

Then, Initiate Rine tried something which seemed a little smarter. He turned Ishtkar around in the air and lifted his staff up high. It seemed to suck in blue light from all around it, and it was soon glowing with an intensity almost as bright as the moon. He opened his mouth and screamed with an energy I never imagined he'd had.

His ice beam hit the demon dragon right on the flank, and it might have shifted the beast by a fraction of a claw. But even trying to cool fire with ice didn't seem to make any difference, as the demon dragon didn't sway from his path.

"*You know nothing,*" I said to Salanraja. "*That's not the best way to taunt something.*"

A rumbling came from Salanraja's chest under my feet, and she let out a deep growl. *"Do you have a better idea?"*

I licked my paw. *"As a matter of fact, I do,"* I said, and I used my superior cat perception to judge Salanraja's current trajectory, as well as the distance between us and the beast and the speed at which both dragons were travelling. Satisfied, I leaped up onto Salanraja's head. *"Get right next to its head. I want to be able to reach."*

"I won't be able to do that without barrelling into it," Salanraja said.

"Then do that," I said.

"Are you going to explain why?"

"No... We have no time."

"Fine. As I said we need to try everything."

Salanraja flapped her wings to get slightly above the demon dragon. From the other side of it, Rine tried sending off another stream of icy energy which this time hit it on the head. But that didn't seem to do anything, either.

Salanraja soon entered a slight dive, and we accelerated towards the demon dragon's head. I crouched down and watched it, ready to swipe at the most opportune moment. Then, I swatted the demon dragon right on the nose with my paw.

Because everyone knew, surely, that there was nothing more annoying than just appearing out of the blue and bashing you in the face. Salanraja then lurched to the right so quickly that I almost fell off of her head. I caught myself on one of the horns sticking out of her neck, and then I pulled myself to safety and retreated into her corridor of spikes.

Meanwhile, the demon dragon turned its head slightly and let out a horrendous roar that seemed to shake both the sky we were in and the earth beneath it. It turned around and followed Salanraja.

"See," I said. *"You don't need magic to get underneath somebody's skin."*

"I've lived through that, since the time I met you," Salanraja replied. She tossed her head around to look at the demon dragon behind her. *"Now, what do we do next?"*

I rushed back towards Salanraja's tail to see the demon dragon right on it. It opened its jaw wide and let out a roar that almost deafened me, I swear. Fires burned from inside its cavernous mouth, as if that great open gap was itself a portal to the Seventh Dimension. *"Fly away,"* I said. *"Fly away very fast."*

"That shouldn't be a problem," Salanraja said, and she flapped her wings hard. She gained a little distance, but then the demon dragon made its counterattack. From its mouth came another roar, and then out came a vortex that was spinning around so fast it engulfed Salanraja's flight path, and we started to get sucked in towards the demon dragon's maw.

"Fly away faster," I instructed. I could feel the tug and the burning, and I couldn't even see the demon dragon now – only the fires that wanted to consume me whole. The wind beat against my fur. I was using my claws to keep a grip on Salanraja's scales. But the pull was so strong that they felt like they were going to rip out of their sockets.

"I can't get any speed," Salanraja said.

"You've got to do something," I replied. *"We'll die otherwise."*

"All in good service," Salanraja said. *"As you said, it's been a good life."*

"No," I replied. *"We can't give up after coming so far."* I looked around for any sign of Initiate Rine. But all I could see was the grey air whirling around me so hard and so fast, and that great raging fire, so hot, so consuming.

"Hang in there, Salanraja," I said, and I crouched, and then leapt upwards as high as I could. I put my whole spine into it, bending backwards, and then I stretched up my paws and extended my claws as far as possible. I found something, and I clung on with all my might. There was a large hole there, in fact two of them, and I soon realised these were the demon dragon's nostrils. I pulled myself up and scrambled onto the demon dragon's head.

Then, I swiped downwards once again at the beast's nose, and it let out another great roar. Instead of eating Salanraja, it swiped at her in the air with its foreleg, sending my dragon tumbling away.

42

SPEAKING THE LANGUAGE

"*S alanraja!*" I cried out in my mind.

I watched her fall for a moment, wanting to dive back down and do something to stop her. The vortex coming out of the demon dragon's mouth had cut off now, and Salanraja fell into a wall of grey and cold clouds. Another cloud hit us dead on, blanketing me in cold and sleety darkness.

"*Salanraja!*" I called again.

No response.

"*Salanraja...*"

"*I'm alive, Ben,*" she said. "*Do what you have to do.*"

Ben... She'd finally called me by my real name. But I didn't have time to dwell on the victory because, just as we emerged from the cloud, the demon dragon let out another roar, and it jerked its head around sharply. I tumbled down its neck, thinking I was going to fall off this thing, then I found myself on the back of the beast. I almost fell right into one of the cracks in its skin, just managing to stop myself with my claws at the very last moment.

These gaps looked even more massive up close. Each one looked like gaps into the centre of the earth, with fires and magma raging beneath. I picked myself up and tried to get my bearings. But the demon dragon shook its body again, and I slid towards another gap. I leapt over it, and turned around, orienting myself.

I ran up the demon dragon's neck again and looked down to see the lake and the beach and Aleam moving on the ground so far below now, I couldn't see what they were doing. I needed to get the demon dragon down there. But it didn't look like the portal was there yet.

"*GET OFF ME, INFIDEL!*" the demon dragon said, and its voice was so loud and booming inside my mind, that I thought for a moment I'd heard it in my ears.

It shook its head again, and this time I dug into the skin with my claws. It wasn't leathery like Salanraja's, instead having the texture of porous rock, and I could feel the intense heat rising from it through the pores in my skin. If I tried staying in place for too long, it would scorch me to death. So, I ran down the demon dragon's neck again, and navigated my way across its back. But it shook its back again, throwing me around like an unwanted child's toy. I found it hard to keep purchase and not fall into any of the cracks.

Initiate Rine on Ishtkar levelled out next to us, and he let off more magic, which this time came out of his staff as a block of ice. It hit the demon dragon right on the side and shattered. Some of the ice went inside its body and rose as steam from the vents. A few of the other shards broke off around me, and one hit me right between the eyes.

"Ouch," I shouted. "That hurt, Rine!" But I wasn't sure whether he heard me. Whiskers, I wasn't sure he even knew I was here.

Then, the demon dragon had the smart idea of rolling, keeping its wings outstretched as it went. It sent me sliding down, and I tried to grasp on with something, but the skin on the wings was smooth like hardened obsidian. I managed to catch myself on some kind of spike that stuck out from the end of it, and from there I dangled. The demon dragon had brought itself down low towards the forest, and he was about to send me smack into a pine tree.

I pivoted out of the way just in time and kept holding on with all my strength, while the dragon lifted me back into the air, going up and up. It lifted me so high my ears wanted to pop. That was when I realised what it was up to. Up there, there wouldn't be enough air for a poor Bengal cat to breathe. But this creature didn't need air, it seemed. Even as it rose, the fires still seemed to rage out of the cracks in its body.

The air became thinner, and my ears hurt even more, and I felt faint. I imagined myself floating even higher in the air, finally carried up by the wings of two beautiful angel cats.

"You can't," a voice came in my head. It wasn't Salanraja. It wasn't the demon dragon. It wasn't Astravar. It was that melodic and lilting female voice that I'd heard in my crystal. *"I gave you your gift for a reason. Trust yourself."*

I hesitated, as I tried to understand exactly what the crystal was getting at. Then, it became clear what I had to do.

I had the gift. The ability to speak to all creatures. I could speak the language of any sentient creature. I could command this demon dragon. *"STOP!"* I screamed out in my mind. I knew the language instinctively. I just needed to work out what to say.

"I AM DEMON DRAGON," it replied in my head. *"THE WARLOCK ASTRAVAR IS MY MASTER... MY PURPOSE IS TO DESTROY ALL LIFE UPON THIS WORLD..."* I wasn't sure whether it was speaking in my mind or out loud anymore. My vision had already gone completely blurry and the world around me was spinning from lack of good air. But I let my instinct guide me. I had to trust something.

"NO," I said. *"I AM YOUR MASTER. NOW, LOWER YOURSELF SO I CAN GIVE YOU YOUR COMMANDS."*

"I AM DEMON DRAGON..." it replied, then it paused a moment as if uncertain. *"I AM DEMON DRAGON... AND DRAGONCAT IS MY MASTER... ASTRAVAR THE DRAGONCAT IS MY MASTER... MY PURPOSE IS UNCERTAIN."*

Well, whatever I'd done, I'd certainly confused it. I held on for dear life, hanging from the horn at the end of the demon dragon's wing. My vision got less bleary, and I could breathe again. I panted hard, and then I checked down below to see Aleam pointing up at me with his staff. Next to him, glared an oval-shaped eye with a white cornea and fire and magma burning within. The portal. Aleam had summoned the portal. Now, all I had to do was bring the demon dragon back to it.

Now, I could hear the demon dragon's primitive thoughts in my own mind, and I knew exactly what Salanraja meant about screaming these thoughts in her mind. Because that is exactly what the demon dragon did.

"*I AM DEMON DRAGON...*" it continued. "*WHO IS MY MASTER? DRAGONCAT... ASTRAVAR... MY FUTURE IS UNCERTAIN...*"

It sounded like it needed a little identity reassurance. "*I AM YOUR MASTER,*" I said in the hideous language of the Seventh Dimension. "*THE WAY BACK TO YOUR WORLD IS NOW OPENED. RETURN AND NEVER COME BACK AGAIN.*"

"*RETURN... PORTAL VISIBLE... ASTRAVAR... I SERVE ASTRAVAR... BUT ALSO DRAGONCAT...*"

I knew that this ruse wouldn't last forever. I didn't have the powerful magic that Astravar had to control this thing. But all I needed to do was fool it for long enough to get it inside.

The demon dragon spiralled downwards towards the portal. As we got even closer, it felt like the portal latched on to us like a vacuum. It was almost as if the Seventh Dimension felt that I belonged in there. Meanwhile, the demon dragon had started to work things out.

"*DRAGONCAT... ASTRAVAR... DRAGONCAT IS AN IMPOSTER... YES, ASTRAVAR.... I HEAR YOU, ASTRAVAR, MY MASTER... DESTROY DRAGONCAT... DESTROY THE WORLD...*"

Whiskers, he'd woken up out of his state. Just as I was about to bring him down to the portal.

"*Just hold him a little longer,*" Salanraja said.

"*I don't know how,*" I said, and it was as if I could feel someone prying inside my own head. Something was trying to stop me speaking, and to take control of my thoughts. It was as if the vengeful eye of Astravar was watching me from inside the portal. I could see it, I swear, hovering above those raging fires. That cruel grey eye that knew nothing of comfort. The one I'd seen in my dreams.

The demon dragon started to lift, as consciousness continued to rouse. At the same time, the portal was closing, and we were so close to being sucked in. But if the demon dragon continued its current course, we would miss the portal by a paw's span.

"Ben," Salanraja said. *"Don't lose control. You can do this."*

Then, I heard the voice of the crystal in my head again. *"Remember your destiny,"* it said. *"You must save the world."*

Those words were enough. The language, the commands, what I needed to do, it came to my mind as clear as lightning. "I, DRAGONCAT, COMMAND YOU!" I screamed, and I screamed it out loud. "RETURN TO THE SEVENTH DIMENSION!"

My thoughts took control of its mind. They snapped on to it, and it felt like I'd leashed invisible reins around the creature's muzzle. The demon dragon's mind suddenly went quiet, and it turned its lumbering form back towards the portal.

I prepared to get sucked in and to join my new world, the Seventh Dimension. I would probably die in there. If everything in there was a demon, then there was absolutely no way I'd find the food I needed to survive. I felt as if I was passing through an incredibly hot waterfall. It seared my skin, and I was prepared to accept my own fate.

"*No, Ben,*" Salanraja said in my mind, and her voice snapped me back to the present. "*Choose life!*"

I screeched and remembered who I was. I wasn't a Dragoncat, whatever a Dragoncat was. I was a Bengal, descendant of the great Asian leopard cat. I was wild, and I was free. Those thoughts gave me enough power in my hind legs to leap off the demon dragon and roll over in the sand.

I turned to face the portal then, the great eye with the raging fires within. It led to a horrific place, one I never wanted to remember seeing, even in nightmares. The demon dragon flew towards a burning sky and then seemed to realise it had been duped. It turned its head, and it looked at me with those empty eyes of fire.

It flew faster in there, or maybe life inside that place was accelerated, because it did a half loop-the-loop and barrel roll within seconds, and for a moment it looked like it would fly right out again. From the direction it was heading, I could tell it wanted to eat me whole.

But Aleam was watching it with one eye, his staff raised as the portal leached energy from a crystal on a pedestal made from a tree trunk. He knocked his staff to the side, to send the crystal toppling to the floor. This cut off the portal just before the demon dragon could emerge.

All that remained was an ear-piercing roar. It sent a massive gust of wind out through the forest, and it shook the trees and brought the sand up from beneath my feet as if it were dust. It whisked it up into suffocating eddies, and it caused the air to howl through the trees. The noises and the crying winds built to a climax as if calling out from the oblivion beneath the world. It screamed out like a massive and very, very angry hippopotamus.

And then, all was still.

I blinked twice, and then I looked back at my fur. It looked charred; it looked beaten. But I was alive, and I couldn't believe it. We'd defeated it. We'd won.

I turned to Aleam, and I meowed and I brushed up next to him. I was purring so loudly, happy just to be alive. He laughed, and he reached out and scratched me under the chin.

"Now," I said. "Maybe Initiate Rine would be so kind as to go out there and catch me a fish." And Ta'ra leapt down from a rock and also looked up at Aleam with wide eyes, as if to tell him she quite fancied fish too.

43

INVISIBLE FISH

I t took a while to return back to Dragonsbond academy, and we took the journey slowly. We had plenty of stop-offs, which gave me time to talk with Rine, Aleam, and Ta'ra about their adventures. They told me about the experiences they'd had throughout the world, and for the first time I gained stories that would make the Savannah cats back in South Wales weep in disbelief.

Salanraja was right, the hippopotamus was nothing compared to the chimera.

We arrived in Dragonsbond Academy later that night, and I'm not sure anyone saw any importance to our return. Aleam suggested that I could spend the night in his study, and Rine seemed to think that was a good idea.

It definitely was a good idea, because the next day I awoke lying on Aleam's sofa, snuggled up next to Ta'ra. I woke naturally, not because of the light, but the delicious aroma of chicken liver coming from two bowls on the floor. They were both white. One had a black cat painted on the front, with a tiny, winged human perched on her shoulder. The other had a cat that didn't look too different from me, with a red dragon flying over his head.

I rushed over to the bowl, purring, and I gobbled up the chicken liver. It tasted so good, and I'd forgotten how much I liked liver. I was so hungry that I was tempted to eat from Ta'ra's bowl as well. It would have been her own fault, really, for wanting to sleep through such a tantalising aroma. But somehow, I resisted. She needed to eat as well, and it took all my willpower, I'm telling you, to pretend that the food wasn't there and to sit in the corner and groom the dust off my fur instead.

Soon, heavy footsteps approached the door. Initiate Rine stood at the entrance. He scanned the room, then his gaze fell on me in the corner. Meanwhile, Ta'ra opened her eyes and yawned.

"Freshcat Ben," Rine said. "You have been called by the Council of Three, and you are to come to see them immediately."

"What do they want?" I asked.

"It doesn't matter," Rine said. "Once the Council summons you, you must come at once."

I looked over at Aleam, who was working away at his alembic apparatus, as if he did anything else. He peered down at me over his glasses. "Initiate Rine is right, I'm afraid," he said. "But once you become an Initiate here, you will be able to apply for a small amount of paid holiday, with the number of days increasing as you rise up the ranks."

I lifted myself up on all fours. "Does that mean I'm about to be promoted?"

Aleam looked at Initiate Rine, and he shook his head. "Just go, will you?" he said. "And don't tell them I said anything."

I stalked towards the door, even if my legs were hurting so much that I thought I would collapse. Aleam had applied some of this so called white magic, but he said it could only cure the bone and it wouldn't soothe the bruises.

I followed Initiate Rine out into the bailey, which was empty. There wasn't a servant, a cat, or even a rat in sight. But after looking around a bit, I noticed a few guards on the *chemin de ronde*, and two stationed by the portcullis.

A light wind rushed through the castle, sending fallen leaves up from the ground. Rine led me across the yard, and then underneath the archway that led to the courtyard.

Which was exactly where the rest of the residents of the castle had gathered, with the exception of Aleam, Ta'ra, the cats in the cattery, and the stationed guards. Everyone had gathered in two clusters, leaving an aisle at the centre which Rine led me through. The servants and the kitchen maids stood at the back, including Matron Canda who turned to regard me with stern eyes. Then we passed the guards, and then the students. Rine's girlfriend, Bellari, was near the aisle, and she backed away from me as I passed, looking down at me with wide eyes. Ange was on the opposite aisle, and she gave me a cute pout, then looked up at Rine and smiled.

Closer to the front, we passed some older dragon riders I'd not even met yet. Some of them looked close to Aleam's age. Prefect Lars and his two friends – Calin and Asinda were also there. But only Asinda turned and looked at me, an expression of mistrust in her narrowed eyes.

We were soon standing right in front of the platform and the lecterns at which the three Driars of the Council of Three – Yila, Lonamm and Brigel – stood in their usual positions. They all had their staffs raised, feeding energy into the crystal. But their gazes were firmly fixed on me.

There came a murmur from the crowd, until Driar Yila raised her free arm and shouted out, "Quiet!" in a voice nearly as loud as a demon dragon's. Then she turned her head sharply toward me and her harsh gaze latched on to mine.

"I hear you've caused quite a commotion, Freshcat," she said. "What do you have to say for yourself?" She banged her staff down against the ground, and I backed up against someone's leg, and hid behind it, remembering what had happened the last time that she'd used that staff's power on me.

Driar Brigel bellowed out a loud and deep laugh from the other side of the platform. "Oh, don't be so cruel to him, Yila," he said. "This pussycat is a hero."

"Indeed, he is," Driar Lonamm said. "Come forward, little one. Don't worry, we won't eat you."

What? Why would they think of eating cats? They didn't do that where I was from. Although I'd heard rumours in my clowder, that they did eat cats on the other side of the world.

I peered out from my hiding place. Driar Lonamm was hunched over her stocky frame and she beckoned me forward. "You'll need to come up to our level if you're to claim your prize," she said, and she tapped on her lectern. "Here, up here."

Well, if I didn't do what they said, they'd probably fry me with their magic. I leaped up, and Driar Lonamm reached out and took something from her pouch. It was a small round disc, connected to some kind of thin chain. It looked just like a cat toy meant for batting around in the air, and I can't imagine it served any kind of functional purpose.

"This is your medal," she said, and she reached out and she placed the thing over my neck.

Yeuch. Collars were bad enough, but this thing felt horrible. I tried to claw it off with my back paws, until Salanraja protested about it in my mind. "*What are you doing, you fool?*"

"*I don't like it.*"

"*Leave it there. It's an honour. You don't want to insult the Council of Three.*"

"*Fine,*" I replied, and I calmed myself down and tried to get used to how wearing this impractical thing impeded my flexibility. Hopefully, I wouldn't have to wear it forever.

Driar Brigel stepped forward, and he stopped the light flowing from his staff to the crystal for a moment, by turning the staff around. He lifted the base and tapped me on each shoulder with it. I flinched, expecting it to hurt. But this man was a lot gentler than he looked.

"Congratulations, Ben," he said. "From this day, you shall be known as Initiate Ben and you will enjoy the full privileges of a student at Dragonsbond Academy. Also, for your heroic deeds, a feast will be made in your honour. Now, let us give our young hero a round of applause."

The humans did that weird thing where they clapped their hands together as if they had suddenly decided they wanted to eliminate a scourge of flies. Some of them even whooped out. Then all went quiet as Driar Yila approached me.

"Much as I hate to do this," she said, not showing any emotion on that cold face, "I am going to give you a grand privilege for your heroic deeds. You, Initiate Ben, shall choose the dish of the day for our feast. Choose wisely, mind, because you can only choose one dish."

Wow. I had never thought I'd have such an honour. Today, I actually got to choose what I had for dinner. I don't think that had ever happened in my life. Of course, the answer was easy.

"I choose salmon," I said.

Driar Yila frowned, and then she looked at Driar Lonamm. "Uh..." she said.

"*Gracious demons,*" Salanraja said. "*Trust you to choose something that doesn't even exist in this world.*"

"*What? You don't have salmon?*" My heart sank, and I suddenly remembered home.

"*And what is a salmon?*"

"*It's a fish, a big one that's pink.*"

There must have been some communication that went on between Salanraja and Great Driar Brigel's dragon, because he immediately boomed out. "I'm sorry, Initiate Ben. But we don't have salmon in this world, and we can't summon one from another dimension."

With that, my heart sank even more. If they couldn't pluck a salmon out of my world, they probably wouldn't be prepared to send me home either. "So, what do you have?" I asked.

"Well, we can offer a rather magical fish," Driar Brigel said. "Something you've never tried before."

My ears perked up. "Really?"

"Yes, it's called Invisible Fish," Lonamm said, raising an eyebrow. "It's quite a delicacy."

"And what's it like?"

Driar Lonamm shook his head with a grin. "I don't know," he said. "In all honesty I've never seen one."

He turned to the crowd and lifted up his arms. The crowd responded with a round of laughter, followed by another round of applause.

EPILOGUE

In the end, we settled on roasted duck as the dish of the day. I had a lot of it, and I even asked Matron Canda to take some over for Ta'ra too, which she did. That night, I slept with contentment. For the first time, I slept in Salanraja's chamber as a celebration for reaching a new rank. I lay curled up next to her chest, where her dragonfire kept me as warm as if I was lying next to the fireplace back in South Wales.

I dreamed strange dreams that night. At the start, I stood peering into a fast-flowing brook. I was looking for fish, as the spray off the water tickled my nostrils, and cooled me against the warmth of the sun. But after a while of finding nothing, I decided that it would be better to dive into the water and find the fish for myself.

So, I plunged into the depths of the river, and the next thing I knew I was swimming upstream, my tail and fins propelling me at great speed. Because I wasn't a cat anymore, I was a fish. In fact, I believe I was a massive salmon swimming my way from the Atlantic Ocean towards our breeding grounds. I had joined a school, and we stayed in close formation. There was safety in numbers should a badger try to fish us out of the water.

But soon, we came to a tributary, and I felt a tug in my head – something telling me to swim in another direction. The rest of the school turned left, but I turned the other way and arrived at a quiet lake, away from the roar and the rush of survival. There was a waterfall in the distance, and I swam towards the bubbles pushing down into the water. Then, once I was close enough, I leapt up into the cascade.

I landed on my feet in a cave behind the waterfall, now a cat again. I shook the water off, then I went on to see what might be inside. There came the squeals of bats, and the cave was lit by a floating light that hovered close to my head, pushing away the darkness. It led me into a chamber, hot like an inferno. Streams of lava seeped down the cave walls, and a white crystal stood at the centre of the chamber.

It glowed brighter as I approached, and I rubbed myself against it to thank it for its help fighting the demon dragon. For a while, my fur brushed against something solid, until the crystal suddenly changed.

I stepped back in alarm, because the crystal had vanished, and Astravar's head instead hovered where it had been. "So, there you are, Dragoncat," he said. "I've been trying to find a way through to you all night."

"What do you want?" I asked. "I defeated you."

"Correction. You sent one of my minions back home. But you will never defeat me, because you are worthless. And you fail to understand now that we warlocks have summoned one demon dragon, we can summon many more."

I tried to ignore him. I didn't want him to ruin my warm feeling of victory. "*Salanraja*," I tried calling out. "*Salanraja, where are you?*"

"She won't help you," Astravar replied. "Not in this dream. Because you chose to come here yourself."

I considered running. But I knew that wherever I fled to, Astravar would find a way to follow me. What I needed to do was wake up, but I had no idea how. "What do you want with me?" I asked Astravar again. "Why are you here?"

"Because I underestimated you," Astravar said. "You can control demons, and that's an incredibly powerful gift. Join me, and we can rule this world together."

The vision that I'd seen of my owners flashed back into my mind.

All three of them lying as skeletons on the bed. I could never let that come to pass. "No," I said. "You are our enemy, and we will find a way to thwart your plans."

Astravar frowned. "I thought you'd say that. Well, it doesn't matter, because I'll find a way through to you one way or another. Believe me, Dragoncat, I will hunt you down and I will make you join me whether you want to or not."

I didn't run. I turned slowly around to send a message to Astravar that I was now in control and could move as I wished. I could hear the roaring of the waterfall somewhere in this cave, and I had to get out from this place – to wake from this dream.

But first, I wanted to return to swimming in the stream, because for a while I could go where I wanted and pretend that I was free.

THE END

But Wait, Not Really...

The story continues in A Cat's Guide to Meddling with Magic, this time with more chimeras than hippopotami.

Visit https://mybook.to/meddlingwithmagic to learn more.

If you wish also to learn more about why Astravar summoned Ben into this world, the short story, *A Cat's Guide to Serving a Warlock*, goes into a little more detail.

You can download it by signing up to my bi-monthly newsletter, where I send information about new releases and I give readers a chance to chime in on writing decisions. New subscribers will also receive a free copy of my Steampunk Fantasy novel, Sukina's Story.

Visit https://chrisbehrsin.com/servingawarlock to subscribe.

Thank you for reading.

ACKNOWLEDGMENTS

The journey to becoming a professional author is a long one, and I wouldn't have travelled so far along it without all the help and the kindness from readers, professionals, friends, and family alike along the way.

Firstly, I'd like to thank Wayne M. Scace for his excellent work editing the manuscript, and Carol Brandon also for her scrupulous proofreading work. Both of you did a wonderful job, and you helped me identify errors that I'd become blind to through being so close to the manuscript.

I'd also like to thank my family, particularly my wife Ola for all the help she gave me working through plot holes and inconsistencies. I'd also like to thank my mother and father for the support they continue to give me through my writing career.

A massive shout out for my ARC team, and all the help that you've given me on this book and my previous works. And finally, I want to express my gratitude for readers and everything that you do to help the publishing and reading communities and the world of literature at large.

ABOUT THE AUTHOR

When Chris Behrsin isn't out exploring the world, he's behind a keyboard writing tales of dragons and magical lands. He was born into the genre through a steady diet of Terry Pratchett. His fiction fuses a love for fantasy and whimsical plots with philosophy and voyages into the worlds of dreams.

Printed in Great Britain
by Amazon

76299505R00125